- Cited by the Guinness Book of World Records as the #1 best-selling writer of all time!

- Author of more than 100 clever, authentic, and sophisticated mystery novels!

- Creator of the amazing Perry Mason, the savvy Della Street, and dynamite detective Paul Drake!

- **THE ONLY AUTHOR WHO OUT-SELLS AGATHA CHRISTIE, HAROLD ROBBINS, BARBARA CARTLAND, AND LOUIS L'AMOUR *COMBINED!***

Why?

Because he writes the best, most fascinating whodunits of all!

You'll want to read every one of them, coming soon from BALLANTINE BOOKS

By Erle Stanley Gardner
Published by Ballantine Books:

The Case of the
Lame Canary

Erle Stanley Gardner

BALLANTINE BOOKS • NEW YORK

Copyright © 1937 by Erle Stanley Gardner
Copyright renewed 1965 by Erle Stanley Gardner

All rights reserved under International and Pan-American
Copyright Conventions. Published in the United States by
Ballantine Books, a division of Random House, Inc., New
York, and distributed in Canada by Random House of
Canada Limited, Toronto.

http://www.randomhouse.com

Library of Congress Catalog Card Number: 95-96147

ISBN 0-345-35162-2

This edition published by arrangement with William Morrow
and Company, Inc.

Manufactured in the United States of America

First Ballantine Books Edition: June 1984

10 9 8 7 6 5 4 3 2 1

CHAPTER ONE

ANY STUDENT of character will concede that outstanding examples of class run contrary to type. The best detectives look like clerks. The best gamblers look like bankers. And nothing in Perry Mason's appearance indicated that his agile brain, unconventional methods, and daring technique made him the city's most feared and respected trial lawyer.

Seated in his office, he regarded the young woman who sat in the big leather chair, holding a caged canary in her lap. His steady eyes held none of the gimlet qualities so frequently associated with cross-examiners, but were, instead, filled with patience, touched with sympathy. His rugged features might have been carved from granite.

"That canary," he said, with the quiet insistence of one who will continue to repeat his statements until he has scored his point, "has a sore foot."

The young woman shifted the cage from her lap to the floor, as though trying to keep the lawyer from seeing too much. "Oh, I don't think so," she said, and then added by way of explanation, "he's a little frightened."

Mason appraised the youthful lines of her figure, the neatly shod feet, the long tapering fingers of the gloved hands. "So," he said, "your business with me was urgent enough to make you crash the gate."

She tilted her chin defiantly. "My business is important. It couldn't wait, and neither could I."

"I take it," the lawyer remarked musingly, "patience isn't one of your virtues."

"I didn't know," she said, "that patience *was* a virtue."

"You wouldn't. What's your name?"

1

"Rita Swaine."

"How old are you, Miss Swaine?"

"Twenty-seven."

"Where do you live?"

"1388 Chestnut Street," she said, glancing across at Della Street, whose pen was busy making copperplate shorthand notes.

"That's all right," Mason assured her, "you needn't worry about Miss Street. She's my secretary. Do you live in an apartment house?"

"Yes. Apartment 408."

"Telephone?"

"Not in my name. There's a switchboard service."

"What do you want to see me about?"

She lowered her eyes and hesitated.

"About the canary?" Mason asked.

"No," she said hastily, "not about the canary."

"Do you usually carry a canary with you?"

She laughed nervously and said, "Of course not. I don't understand why you attach so much importance to the canary."

"Because," he told her, "so few of my clients bring canaries to the office."

She started to say something, then checked herself. Mason glanced significantly at his wrist watch and his action started her talking. "I want you to help my sister, Rossy," she said. "That's short for Rosalind. About six months ago she married Walter Prescott. He's an insurance adjuster, and he married her for her money. He manipulated things so he got most of it and—and now he's trying to make trouble for Rossy."

"What sort of trouble?" Mason asked as she hesitated.

"Trouble over Jimmy."

"Who's Jimmy?"

"Jimmy Driscoll. She was going with him before she married Walter."

"And Driscoll's still in love with her?" Mason asked.

She shook her head emphatically and said, "No. Jimmy's in love with *me*."

"Then why should your sister's husband—"

"Well, Jimmy wrote her a letter, as a friend."

"What sort of a letter?"

"Rosalind started it. She wrote to Jimmy and told him she was unhappy, and Jimmy wrote to her, just as a friend, and advised her to break away from Walter. He said Walter had only married her for her money, and that marriage was just like a financial investment, your first loss was your best loss. You see," she went on with a nervous laugh, "Jimmy's in the brokerage business and handled Rosalind's investments for her before her marriage, so she'd understand what he meant by that sort of talk."

"He didn't handle her investments after marriage?"

"No."

"And Walter Prescott got this letter Driscoll wrote?"

"That's right."

Mason's face showed his interest. "And," the girl in the pearl-gray suit went on quickly, "I don't think Rossy knows how Jimmy feels toward me. You see, we never mention his name. But I have some money of my own, and, after Rossy's marriage, Jimmy kept right on handling *my* investments, and I went out with him quite a bit."

"And your sister knows nothing of this?"

"No—at any rate, I don't think so."

"What's Prescott going to do about the letter?" Mason asked.

"He's going to sue Rossy for divorce, claiming that she's kept up her old affair with Jimmy. And he's going to sue Jimmy for alienation of affections because he put in the letter about Walter's marrying her for her money and told her she'd better leave him."

Mason shook his head. "I don't handle divorce cases."

"Oh, but you *must* handle this. I haven't told you everything yet."

Mason glanced quizzically across at Della Street, smiled and said, "Well, then, suppose you tell me everything."

"Walter got about twelve thousand dollars from Rossy.

He said he was going to invest it in his business and she'd get better than ten percent on her money, and the investment would increase in value. Now he swears he never received a cent from her."

"Can she prove that he did?"

"I'm afraid not. You know how it is with things like that. A woman certainly wouldn't ask her husband to give her a receipt. Rosalind had some bonds and she gave them to Walter and told him to sell them and put the money in the business. Walter admits he sold some securities for her, but he claims the money was turned over to her. And George Wray, that's Walter's partner —Prescott & Wray in the Doran Building, Insurance Adjusters—says it's absurd to think that Walter put any such amount of money in the business. He says they've been taking money *out* of the business instead of putting it *in*.

"So you see what's happening. Walter's got that money and he's trying now to put Rossy in the wrong so he can get away with it."

"Yes," Mason told her, "I think you'd better see some good lawyer who specializes in domestic relations and . . ."

"No. No. We want *you*. You see— Well, something happened this morning."

Mason smiled at her and said, "Now listen, young lady, I'm not interested in divorce cases. I like trial work. I specialize in murder cases. I like mysteries. I sympathize with your sister, but I'm *not* interested in her case. There are hundreds of competent attorneys in the city who will be glad to represent her."

The young woman's lips trembled. "I w-w-w-wish you'd at least hear what I have to s-s-s-say," she said, blinking back tears. But, apparently recognizing the futility of her appeal, she hooked the middle finger of her right hand through the ring in the wire cage, and prepared to arise from the big leather chair.

Mason said, "Wait a minute. I'm interested in that canary. Odd things like that stick in my mind. Now, I want to know *why* you carried that canary into my office."

"That's what I wanted to t-t-tell you. I was working up to it in my own w-w-w-way."

"Go ahead and tell me," Mason said, "and then perhaps I can forget it. Otherwise I'll be wasting the entire afternoon speculating on the thing, trying to uncover some logical explanation."

"Well," she said, "I was over at Rosalind's house this morning, cutting the canary's claws with a nail clipper. You know, a canary in a cage has to have the tips clipped off his claws every so often. And while I was doing that, Jimmy came—and told me he loved me, and took me in his arms, and the canary got away—and then two automobiles smashed into each other right in front of the house— And I looked up at the window, and there was Mrs. Snoops watching us, and a man was hurt in the automobile accident, and Jimmy ran out, and the officers got his name and license number, and Jimmy will be called as a witness when they try the automobile damage case, and Walter will say that Jimmy came to his h-h-h-house without his c-c-consent, and— And— Dammit! I hate to b-b-b-bawl, and you've made me c-c-cry."

She snapped open her purse, fished out a square of scented lace and jabbed furiously at the tears which oozed from her eyes.

Mason settled back in his chair with a deep sigh of contentment. "An automobile accident, a love story, a lame canary, and Mrs. Snoops. What could be better? Something seems to tell me that I'm going to take your sister's case. At any rate, I'm going to hear all about it. Now quit crying and tell me about Mrs. Snoops."

Rita Swaine blew her nose, tried to smile away her tears, and said, "I hate to cry. Usually I take things on the chin. Don't think I put on an act to impress you, Mr. Mason, because I didn't."

He nodded and said, "Who's Mrs. Snoops?"

"We call her Mrs. Snoops because she's such an old busybody. Her name's Stella Anderson. She's a widow who has the house next door, and she's always snooping and prying into other people's business."

"And Jimmy told you he loved you?"

"Yes."

"And this was over at Rosalind's house?"

"Yes."

"How did Jimmy happen to come there to tell you he loved you, and where was Rosalind?"

"Well," she said, drying the last of her tears, "Walter found Jimmy's letter and started making an awful scene. He went to see his lawyer and Rossy was afraid he was going to do something terrible. He'd threatened to kill her, and Rossy thought he might do it. She wanted to leave right away. So she ran out of the house and was afraid to go back."

"What time was that?"

"I don't know exactly what time. It was early this morning, around nine or ten o'clock, I think. Well, anyway, a little after eleven, Rossy telephoned me and told me what had happened, and asked me to go over to the house and pack up her clothes in her wardrobe trunk and a couple of suitcases which were in the closet of her bedroom. You see, her house is over at 1396 Alsace Avenue. Walter bought it just before they were married. It's only a couple of blocks from where I live."

"You have a key to the house?" Mason asked.

She shook her head.

"How did you get in, then?"

"Oh," she said, "Rossy just ran out and left the doors unlocked. Walter said he was going to kill her, and she was frightened."

"And the canary?" Mason asked.

"It's her canary. She's had it for years. She wanted me to keep it for her. Walter would have killed it just out of spite. That's how mean he is. He'll be simply furious when he returns and finds her gone."

Mason said, "I'm sorry. I should have let you walk out, then I could have indulged in a lot of speculation as to what combination of circumstances had forced a frightened young woman to carry a caged canary through the streets and into my office. Now you've explained a perfectly intriguing mystery into an uninteresting commonplace."

Her eyes showed indignation.

"I'm so sorry I bored you, Mr. Mason!" she blazed. "After all, my sister's happiness doesn't mean a thing as compared with *your* entertainment!"

The lawyer smiled and shook his head. "Don't get me wrong," he explained. "I'm going to see you through. That's the price I'll pay for indulging my curiosity. So go ahead and tell me the rest of it."

"You mean you're going to represent her?"

Mason nodded.

Her face showed relief. "That's splendid of you."

"Not at all," Mason said wearily. "I became interested in that canary. The only legitimate reason I had to pry into your private affairs was as your attorney. So I made my decision and will pay the price. The fact that I'm about to embark on a distasteful case naturally needn't concern you. So Jimmy Driscoll told you he loved you, did he?"

She nodded.

"Had he ever told you that before?" Mason asked, watching her shrewdly.

"No," she said, "never before." And her eyes dropped down to rest on the caged canary.

"But you knew it, of course," Mason went on.

"Well, not exactly," she said in a low voice. "I knew that I liked him and I hoped he liked me. But it came as a surprise."

"And how," Mason asked, "did it happen that Jimmy Driscoll came over to Rosalind's house?"

She lifted her eyes to his, then, and said, "He went to my apartment first. The clerk at the desk over there thinks Jimmy is just about right. Jimmy was able to make him a little money once, so the clerk told him that my sister had called and seemed very much excited and that I'd dashed over to her house in a hurry."

"He'd been listening in on the wire?" Mason asked.

"No, I don't think so. He knows Rossy's voice, so he knew she'd called, and then when I left I told him where I was going."

"So Jimmy went over to Rosalind's house?"

"Yes. You see, it's only a couple of blocks."

"And found you there?"

"Yes."

"And you told him Rossy had left?"

"Yes."

"And then what happened?"

Once more her eyes avoided the lawyer's.

"Well," she said, "we talked for a while, and I was holding the canary in my hand and clipping his claws, and then the first thing I knew Jimmy's arms were around me, and he told me how he loved me, and I let go of the canary and clung to him. And then, while I was trying to catch this canary, all of a sudden there was this terrible crash out in front of the house, and, naturally, we ran to the living room window—we were in the solarium at the time—and found this big covered moving van and a coupe had had a smash-up, and of course the coupe had got the worst of it. The driver was hurt, and Jimmy ran out to help lift the driver out of the coupe. The driver of the van said he could rush the man to the hospital quicker than waiting for an ambulance, so he and Jimmy loaded him in the van."

"Then Jimmy came back into the house?" Mason asked.

She nodded.

"And what happened after that?"

"Well, we talked things over, and I decided perhaps he'd better leave, because Walter was going to make trouble and I didn't think it would be a good thing for people to know Jimmy had been there in the house. I thought he might be called as a witness to that automobile accident. You see, he'd parked his car on the side street and I thought perhaps the driver of the van would come back and try to involve Jimmy in some way. And

Mrs. Snoops had been watching us when Jimmy took me in his arms, and—"

"So Jimmy left the house?"

"Yes. But Mrs. Snoops must have telephoned for the police when the accident happened, because when Jimmy walked out of the house, he walked right into the arms of a couple of officers who'd driven up in a radio car. They asked questions about the accident and took Jimmy's name and address. They made him show them his driving license so he *had* to give them his right name."

"What time was this?" Mason asked.

"It must have been two or three hours ago. I think it was right about noon when the accident happened."

"What time did Rosalind call you?"

"Around ten or eleven o'clock, I think—I can't tell exactly."

"Well," Mason said, "if you want me to represent your sister in the divorce action, you'd better have her come in and talk with me."

Rita Swaine nodded, leaned across the arm of the chair and spoke rapidly. "Yes, that's all right, Mr. Mason, I'll have her do that, but don't you think it would be a good plan to fix things so we could keep Walter from ever finding out that Jimmy was there at the house? You see, Rosalind left this morning and Walter might make it appear that Jimmy had something to do with her leaving."

"But Jimmy is in love with *you*," Mason said.

She nodded.

"Well, then," Mason said, "why not simply come out and say so? Why not announce your engagement?"

"Because," she said, "people would think it was something Jimmy, Rosalind and I had cooked up to keep Walter from getting anywhere with his case."

Mason's eyes narrowed. "So you've thought of *that*, have you?"

"Why," she said, "it seems to me the logical thing for Walter's lawyer to claim. So I thought perhaps you could investigate this accident, and if the man in the coupe

was in the wrong, fix it so he didn't sue, and if the driver
of the van was responsible, see that they made a prompt
settlement so there wouldn't be any lawsuit. Then it
wouldn't come out that it was Jimmy who was there in
the house."

"How seriously was the man injured?" Mason asked.

"I don't know. He was unconscious when Jimmy helped
load him in the van."

"Do you know who owned the van?"

"Yes, there was a sign. It's 'Trader's Transfer Company.' "

"How about the coupe?"

"It's still out in front," she said, "pretty badly smashed.
The license number is 6T2993, and the registration certificate wrapped around the steering post shows that it's
registered in the name of Carl Packard, who lives at
1836 Robinson Avenue, Altaville, California."

Mason nodded, turned to Della Street and said, "Ring
the Drake Detective Agency, Della. Ask Paul Drake to
step in here." Then to Rita Swaine, "I'll get busy right
away and see what can be done about that automobile
accident. In the meantime, you tell your sister to come in
and see me."

"I don't know just *where* Rossy is right now," she said,
"but as soon as I hear from her I'll tell her to come in."

"Where can I reach you?" Mason asked.

"I'll be at my apartment."

The lawyer glanced across at his secretary. "You have
the address, Della?"

"Yes," Della Street said. "What's your telephone number, Miss Swaine?"

"Ordway six-naught-nine-two-two."

Mason arose, crossed the office, and opened the corridor door.

"Isn't there a retainer to be paid now?" Rita Swaine
asked, opening her purse and pulling out a sheaf of
currency.

"Now now," Mason told her. "After all, you know, I
asked for this. . . . And you'd better put that money in

the bank, young lady. Good Lord! You don't carry sums like that around in your purse, do you?"

"Of course not. I thought you'd want some money before you went ahead with the case, so I stopped at the bank and got two thousand dollars."

Mason started to say something, then smiled, held the door open for her and said, "Well, you'd better put it back in the bank, Miss Swaine. I'll fix a fee later on when I feel more generous. Right now I can only think of you as a young woman who spoiled a mystery. Good afternoon."

"Good afternoon, Mr. Mason," she said. She put the money back in her purse, picked up the canary cage and walked rapidly from the office. In the corridor she paused to inquire, "Do you know anything about the pet store that's in this block?"

"The man who runs it," Mason said, "was once a client of mine. He's an old German, quite a character. Karl Helmold's the name. Why did you ask?"

"I thought I'd leave Dickey there for a while."

"That's the canary?"

"Yes. Then, when Rossy gets settled she can send for him. But I'd want to be certain that Walter wouldn't know where I'd left him."

"I'm quite sure," Mason said, "you can trust the discretion of Karl Helmold. Tell him I sent you."

She nodded, and her clacking heels echoed rapid steps as she walked toward the elevator.

Mason closed the door and turned to Della Street.

"That," he said, making a wry grimace, "is what comes of trying murder cases. I'm constantly translating everyday occurrences into terms of the bizarre. That girl came in here carrying a caged canary. She was excited, nervous and upset, and I, like a fool, began to clothe her with all sorts of mysterious backgrounds."

"Why didn't you refuse to take her case, Chief?" Della Street asked.

"Not after I'd pried into her private affairs, Della. Remember, this is just a business with us. It's something else to the client. The sister's divorce case is a chore to me, but right now it's the most important thing in that young woman's life—except her love affair with Jimmy Driscoll."

Della Street surveyed the lawyer with thoughtfully speculative eyes. "Chief," she said, "speaking to you as a woman who is under no illusions as to her sex, and is, therefore, immune to feminine wiles and tearful entreaties, did it occur to you there's something strange about the way she reacted to that love affair? She wouldn't look you in the eyes when she talked about it. She acted as though it were something furtive, something to be concealed, something of which she was ashamed. Don't you think that she may have doublecrossed her sister more than she admits—in order to get Jimmy, I mean?"

Mason chuckled delightedly and said, "There *you* go, Della. I tell you, it's too many murder cases. First it's a caged canary which throws *me* for a loss, then this love affair gets *you*. What we need's a vacation. What do you say we chuck the whole business and take a trip around the world? I'll look into the jurisprudence of the different countries we visit, and you can take notes on what I find."

Her eyes widened. "You mean it, Chief?"

"Yes."

"How about the law business?"

"We'll leave it. Jackson can handle routine matters while I'm gone, and there'll be plenty of big things when we get back."

"And how about *this* case?"

"Oh," Mason said casually, "we'll get Rossy out of her difficulties. That won't take long."

Della Street picked up the telephone and said to the exchange operator in the outer office, "Get me the Dollar Steamship Company on the line. Right away, please, before the boss changes his mind."

CHAPTER TWO

PAUL DRAKE, head of the Drake Detective Agency, braced his tall, thin form languidly against the door jamb. The film which covered his slightly protruding eyes seemed like a veil drawn between his thoughts and the outer world. During moments of repose, his fish-like mouth hung partially open, giving his face an expression of droll humor. Even an acute observer would have admitted he looked more like a drunken undertaker than a detective.

"My God, Perry," he said, in drawling protest, "don't tell me you're starting on another case."

Mason nodded.

"I wish," Drake went on in the same good-natured, drawling voice, "that *you'd* take a vacation for *my* health."

"What's the matter, Paul? Can't you take it any more?"

Drake sauntered over to the big leather chair, sat down in it cross-wise, one of the chair's arms supporting his back, the other catching his legs just back of the knees. "I've known you now for five years," he said reproach-fully, "and I never saw you yet when you weren't in a hurry."

"Well," Mason told him crisply, "I'm not going to break the record now, Paul. Some time around noon, out near the corner of Fourteenth Street and Alsace Avenue, a truck owned by the Trader's Transfer Company smashed a coupe driven by Carl Packard of Altaville, California. It should be a cinch to chase down. Packard was injured, and the truck driver put him in the van and rushed him to a hospital. Find out which hospital, how seriously

13

Packard was hurt, whether he's insured, whether the truck's insured, how the truck driver reported the accident, whether the trucking company will admit liability, and how much the case can be settled for by whichever party was in the wrong."

Drake said, "And you want all of this in a hurry?"

"Yes. I'd like to have the information in an hour."

"And that's all you want?"

"No. Here's another one. Walter Prescott, 1396 Alsace Avenue, suing his wife for divorce. Find out who his girl-friend is."

"What makes you think he has one?"

"He short-changed his wife out of twelve thousand bucks. He didn't put it in his business."

"Any leads?" Drake asked.

"Nothing in particular. He's an insurance adjuster. The firm name is Prescott & Wray, and they have offices in the Doran Building. Find out where he buys his flowers. Get a look at the delivery addresses at the florist's. Have an operative bust into Prescott's office and claim that a young woman driving Prescott's automobile smashed into him and ripped off a fender and hasn't settled. Watch what number he calls up when he refutes the story. Put a couple of shadows on him and find where he goes when he isn't at the office."

"Suppose he's wise and doesn't go?"

"Write him an anonymous letter that his sweetie has another boy-friend who calls on her every afternoon. Start him moving around, then see where he moves to."

Drake pulled a leather-covered notebook from his pocket and wrote names and addresses.

"Here's something else," Mason said. "A Stella Anderson has the house next door to the Prescott place. Apparently she's the neighborhood gossip. Drop in and kid her along. See if she can't give you a line on Prescott. Find out whether he spends his evenings home or is out a good part of the time and see if she dishes out any dirt on Prescott's wife."

"In other words," Drake said mournfully, "you want everything."

"That's it," Mason told him. "Put some operatives out doing the leg work. You'd better talk with Mrs. Snoops first, and then pull the rough stuff to make Prescott contact his girl-friend. You can write him an anonymous letter and send it special delivery. Put a couple of shadows on him—"

"Who's the Snoops dame?" Drake asked.

Mason grinned. "I forgot about that. That's a pet name for the Anderson woman."

"Anything else?"

"Yes. While you're getting the low-down on the neighborhood gossip from Mrs. Anderson, find out about a necking party which she looked in on next door some time this morning."

"What do you want me to find out about it?"

"Just get her description of it," Mason said. "It sounds just a little fishy to me."

"Don't people neck in the mornings in that neighborhood?" Drake asked.

"It isn't that. It's just the way the thing was described to me. Okay, Paul, on your way."

"How many men shall I turn loose on this thing?"

"All you need to get results in a hurry."

"Any limit on expenses?"

"No limit," Mason said. "This is my party."

"What's the idea? Getting benevolent?"

"No. I fell for a lame canary and what I thought was a mystery. This is what comes of it."

"Sounds like a goofy case," Drake said, pivoting around in the chair and getting to his feet.

"It is."

"Okay. You want me to report by telephone?"

"Uh huh. Keep feeding stuff in to me as soon as you get it. If I'm not here, you can talk with Della. I'm going out and see a man."

"About a dog?" Drake asked, grinning.

"About a canary."

The detective frowned, "What's the gag about the canary, Perry?"

"I don't know. Tell me, Paul, why should a canary have a sore foot?"

"I'll bite," Drake countered. "Why should it?"

Mason motioned toward the door. "On your way," he said. "You're no help at all."

The detective heaved an exaggerated sigh. "This," he announced, "is a relief."

"What is?" the lawyer asked.

"Because you didn't want me to shadow the canary," Drake said. "I was afraid you were going to turn him loose, ask me to get an airplane, a pair of binoculars, and submit a complete report on him from egg to cage."

He opened the door a few inches and eased himself almost furtively into the corridor, his grin fading through the narrow opening as he silently pulled the door to.

Mason reached for his hat, said, "I'm going down to the pet store, Della."

"Still worrying about the canary, Chief?"

He nodded. "*Why* should a canary have a sore foot? Why should a girl carry a canary through the streets and up to a law office?"

"Because her sister wants the canary put in a safe place."

Mason said slowly, "Looks like her sister intends to be away for a while. And, when you come right down to it, Della, no one has told us where the sister is right now."

"She said she didn't know," Della Street explained.

"That," Mason told her, "is exactly my point. Damn it, don't *you* take all the romance out of life. If I can squeeze a mystery out of this canary, I'm going to do it —even if I have to put him through a clothes wringer."

CHAPTER THREE

THE PET STORE on the corner was a bedlam of noise when Mason opened the door, nodded to a clerk, and walked back toward the office in the rear. A parrot screeched greeting. A chained monkey thrust forth an inquisitive paw, clutching at the lawyer's coat. A fat individual, with pale, patient eyes, and a black skullcap protecting the shiny dome of an onion bald head, looked up from a ledger, then came waddling from the glass-enclosed office.

"*Ja, Ja,*" he said, "it is the *Herr* Counselor, himself! It is an honor you come to my place of business."

Mason shook hands, perched himself on the edge of a counter and said, "I haven't much time, Karl. I want to find out something."

"*Ja, ja!* About the *Fräulein* who came in with the canary, eh? She said that you had sent her. You perhaps want to know something about that canary?"

Mason nodded.

"It is a good canary," Helmold said. "It is worth a good price. He has a fine voice."

"He seems to have a sore foot," the lawyer said.

"*Ja.* It is nothing. The claws on the right foot have been cut too short. Today he is lame. Tomorrow he is lame. The next day, nothing. And the day after that, you could never tell."

"How about the left foot?" Mason asked.

"On the left foot the claws are cut nicely, all except one claw, and that claw, it is not cut at all. I do not understand."

17

"The claws were cut today?" Mason asked.

"*Ja, ja.* There are little fine threads of blood on the perch which come from the sore toes of the right foot. It was done today, *ja.*"

"And the young woman wants to keep him here?"

"*Ja.*"

"For how long?"

The fat proprietor of the pet store shrugged his shoulders and said, "I do not know. She does not tell me that."

"For a day?" Mason asked.

The eyes grew wide with surprise. "You joke, *nicht wahr?* A day! What sort of a storage business is that?"

"No," Mason said, "I want to know. Did she say anything about leaving him here for a day?"

"*Ach,* no. By the month I quoted her prices, and by the month she paid. Understand, Counselor, not even by the week; by the month."

Mason slid from the counter. "Okay, Karl," he said. "I just wanted to check up on it."

"I thank you for sending her to me," Helmold said. "Some day perhaps I can do something for you, *nicht wahr?*"

"Possibly," Mason said. "What name did she give you?"

"Her name?"

"Yes."

Helmold stepped into the office, thumbed over some records, came out with a card in his hand and said, "The name is Mildred Owens, and the address is General Delivery, Reno. She moves to Reno, and after a while she sends and gets the bird. But not for more than a month, anyway."

A slow grin spread over the lawyer's face.

"That is good news?" Helmold asked anxiously, looking over the top of his glasses.

"Very good news," Mason said. "You know, Karl, I was commencing to think my hunches weren't right. Now I feel a lot better. Take care of that canary, Karl."

"*Ja, ja.* I take care of him. Would you like to look around and—"

"Not today, Karl. I'll see you some other time. I'm busy right now."

Helmold nodded genially, escorted Perry Mason to the door of the pet shop. "Any time I can do something for you, you tell me. It is a pleasure. This—" with a sweep of his hand—"talk of a lame canary, it is nothing. I wish to do something."

Mason grinned, left the pet-shop proprietor bowing and smiling in the doorway, and sought a barber shop, where he was shaved, massaged and manicured.

Usually, hot towels on his face made him relax into a state where he was neither awake nor asleep, a peculiar, drowsy, half-dreaming condition in which, his imagination stimulated, he could see things with crystal clarity. But this time the hot towels steamed no thoughts into his mind. The canary was lame. One of the claws on the left foot had not been clipped at all. The remaining claws on that foot had been trimmed correctly. But the claws on the right foot had been trimmed too closely. And it was this which made the canary lame. Moreover, Rita Swaine, in taking the bird to the pet store, had been frank enough in referring to Mason as the person who had sent her there, but had given a fictitious name and address.

Why?

Out of the barber chair, Mason adjusted his tie, glanced at his wrist watch, and strolled leisurely back to his office. The street was filled with afternoon shadows and the advance guard of the late afternoon traffic jams.

Rounding the corner in the corridor from the elevator, he saw Della Street standing in the doorway of his private office, beckoning to him frantically, and, as he quickened his stride, she ran swiftly down the flagged floor of the building.

"Listen," she said, "Paul Drake's on the private line and he says he must talk with you *right* away."

Mason's long legs added another few inches to his quick stride. "How long ago did he call?"

"He's on the line, just this minute. I recognized the sound of your steps in the corridor."

"This his first call?"

"Yes."

Mason said, "It may be important, Della. Don't go home until we find out." He pushed his way into his private office, picked up the receiver of his desk telephone and said in a low voice, "Okay, Paul, what is it?"

The slightly distorted sound of the detective's voice showed the lawyer that Drake was holding his lips directly against the transmitter.

"Perry," he said, "was this a run-around?"

"Was what a run-around?"

"About the divorce case."

"No. What are you talking about?"

"I think," Drake told him, "you'd better get out here right away."

"Where's 'here'?"

"Out in front of Mrs. Stella Anderson's place on Alsace Avenue. I'm talking from a drug store a couple of blocks away, but I'll meet you where my car's parked."

"What's the trouble?" Mason asked, frowning.

Drake lowered his voice and said, "Listen. A couple of men in a prowl car drove up, stopped at the Prescott house, opened the back door with skeleton keys, and went in. About fifteen minutes later, Sergeant Holcomb of the homicide squad came out with lots of sirens and a couple of men, and a few minutes later the coroner showed."

Mason gave a low whistle. "Did you pick up anything, Paul?"

"Not much, but I understand the tip-off came from a Mrs. Weyman, who lives just west of the Prescott house on Fourteenth Street."

"How did she get the tip-off?" Mason asked.

"No one knows."

"And you don't know who's the corpse."

"No."

"You," Mason told him, "wait for me in front of Stella Anderson's place. I'm coming out. And let me give you a tip, Paul—don't ever underestimate a hunch on a lame canary."

CHAPTER FOUR

DRAKE'S AUTOMOBILE was parked near a neat, but somewhat dingy-looking house, just to the north of a big two-storied residence in front of which half a dozen cars were clustered.

Mason slid his car to a stop in behind Drake's machine. The detective joined him on the sidewalk. "They know you're here, Paul?"

"Not yet. They haven't spotted me."

"Have they started asking questions of the neighbors?"

"Not yet. They're fooling around inside the house."

"Newspaper men?"

"Yes, a couple of those cars are Press. I got the low-down on the Weyman tip-off from one of them."

"Okay," Mason said, "we haven't much time. Let's go. You make a stab at Mrs. Weyman, pretend you're selling washing machines, life insurance, or investigating the auto accident. I'll take Mrs. Snoops. Join me here. Make it snappy."

Drake nodded, swung around the corner. Mason walked up a narrow cement walk, climbed the echoing steps of a wooden porch, and pressed his thumb against the bell button. He had rung the third time when the door was thrown open and an angular woman, whose long, bony nose fenced apart restless, glittering eyes, asked impatiently, "What do you want?"

"I'm investigating an automobile accident which took place out here—"

"Come in," she said. "Come right in. Are you a detective?"

Mason shook his head.

For a moment there was a flicker of disappointment on her face, but she led the way into an old-fashioned living room where chairs with crocheted doilies for head and arm rests were arranged in a stiffly conventional design.

"Sit down," she invited. "—Land sakes, I'm so excited I'm all of a tremble, what with that automobile accident this morning, and then what they've found over in the Prescott house. I just can't seem to calm myself down."

Mason seated himself, stretched his neck to peer out of the window. "What have they found in the Prescott house?" he asked.

"I don't know," she said, "but I *think* it's a murder. And I don't know whether I did right in not telling the officers what I saw. I suppose they'll come over and question me, won't they?"

Mason smiled and said, "What *did* you see, Mrs. Anderson?"

"Well," she said, sitting very stiffly erect, "I saw plenty. I just said to myself, says I to myself, says I, 'There's something going on over in that house, and you, Stella Anderson, had better call the officers.' "

"But you didn't do it?"

"Not about that. I called them about the automobile accident."

"And you didn't tell them about what you'd seen in the house?"

She shook her head, compressed her thin lips and said in a tone of righteous indignation, "They didn't ask me. They didn't even come near the house. I never had a chance to tell them, and it serves them right!"

"What!" Mason exclaimed. "They didn't even come to talk with you after you'd put in the call for them?"

"That's right. They came and looked over that coupe, and took down the license number and copied the registration certificate, then they talked with the young man who came out of Walter Prescott's house, and then got in their car and drove away. They never once came near my place, not once!"

"And you'd seen something you could have told them about?" Mason asked.

"I'll say I could."

Mason, sizing her up with his steady, patient eyes, crossed one leg over the other, settled back in the chair and said casually, "Oh, well, if it had been important they'd have asked you about it."

She teetered back and forth on the edge of her chair, her bony back rigid with indignation. "What's that?" she snapped.

Mason said, "They probably had all the information about the automobile accident they needed."

"Well," she said, bristling, "it just happens this wasn't about the automobile accident. Don't you go jumping at conclusions, young man."

Mason raised his eyebrows. "What was it?"

"No," she said, "it doesn't concern you. You're investigating the automobile accident. What do you want to know about it?"

"Everything *you* know about it," Mason said.

"Well," she said, "I was here in my house at the time."

"Did you actually see the accident?"

Her face showed disappointment. "I heard the sound of sliding tires and ran to the window just about the time of the crash. The cars were locked together and skidding. Then they struck the curb with an awful crash. The man who was driving the van jumped down and tried to get the door of the coupe open, but he couldn't do it. Then he ran around to the other side of the coupe, and by that time the man had run out of the Prescott house. He helped—"

"What man?" Mason interrupted her.

"A man I'd seen over there earlier."

Mason raised his eyes and said, "Oh, you *had* seen him, then."

"Of course I'd seen him."

"You didn't say so."

"Well, you didn't give me a chance."

"I thought," Mason remarked, "that I'd asked you about what you saw in the house and you told me it was none of my business— Do you mind if I smoke?"

"I didn't say it was none of your business," she said, "and I'd very much prefer you didn't smoke. The odor of tobacco gets in the curtains and stays there."

Mason nodded. "Where were you when you first heard the sound of sliding tires?"

"I was in the dining room," she said.

Mason nodded to an open archway and said, "That's the room?"

"Yes."

"Would you," Mason asked, "mind showing me exactly where you were standing?"

She got to her feet with effortless agility and without bending her back. Without a word, she strode through the doorway into the dining room.

"Stand just as you were standing when you heard the sound of the tires," Mason said.

She turned and stared out through the south window. Mason stepped over and stood at her side. "That's the Prescott house over there?" he asked.

"Yes."

"You're rather close to it, aren't you?"

"Yes."

"What's the room directly opposite?"

"That's the solarium."

"And you were standing here when you heard the sound of the tires?"

"Yes."

"In just about this position?"

"Yes."

"And what did you do?"

"I ran through that door, across the parlor, pulled back the curtains and looked out."

"Just in time to see the van push the coupe into the curb?"

"Yes."

"Do you," Mason asked, "know who was to blame?"

"No. I didn't see enough of it. And, even if I had, I might not be able to tell much. I never did learn to drive a car. Now, let's go back in the other room. There's something I'm interested in, and—"

"What did you do after the accident?"

"Well, I went to my telephone and notified the police there'd been an accident and a man was hurt. After a few minutes, a police car came around that corner. The young man who had helped load the driver of the coupe in the truck was just leaving the Prescott house. The men from the police car asked him questions and made him show them his driving license—"

She broke off as a car drove by on Alsace Avenue. She followed it with her eyes until it slowed and rounded the corner on Fourteenth Street.

"That's seven cars," she said, "that have come there in the last half hour. Now, who do you suppose *that* could be?"

"I'm sure I don't know," Mason told her.

"Well, one of the cars had 'Homicide Squad' painted on the side. You could hear the siren coming a mile away."

Mason said, "Perhaps the man who was hurt in the automobile accident died."

"Don't be silly," she snapped. "The man who was hurt went to a hospital. Traffic accidents aren't homicides. This was the homicide squad."

"Are you," Mason asked, "absolutely certain that the young man ran out of the Prescott house?"

"Of course I'm certain."

"Isn't it possible he'd been sitting in a car parked around the corner? I see that the Prescott house is right on the corner of Fourteenth Street and—"

"Certainly not," she interrupted. "That's absurd! I guess I know when a man comes out of a house. What's more, I saw him in the house *before* that accident."

Mason raised inquiring eyebrows. "Whatever happened in the Prescott house couldn't have any bearing on the automobile accident. I'm afraid you've exaggerated some trivial neighborhood happening—"

"Fiddlesticks!" she interrupted. "Now you look here, young man— What's your name?"

"Mason."

"All right, Mr. Mason, you look here. I know when something's important and when it isn't. Now you let me tell you just what I saw over there, and you'll realize that it *is* important and what a mistake those radio officers made not coming over to talk with me in the first place.

"Now, I was standing in front of that window in my dining room, looking out. I wasn't looking at anything in particular, but you can see how things are. A body can't help but see things that go on in the solarium over in the Prescott house unless the shades are drawn. And Mrs. Prescott never draws the shades. Land sakes, the things I've seen— Well, this young man was in there with Mrs. Prescott's sister. She was *alone* in that house with this young man."

"He probably just dropped in to pass the time of day," Mason said.

Her sniff was eloquent. "The time of day," she exclaimed scornfully. "Well, he'd been there exactly forty-two minutes before the accident, and if you'd seen what I saw when Rita Swaine let go of that canary you'd change your tune a bit."

"What," Mason asked, striving to keep the interest from his voice, "caused her to let go of the canary?"

"She was standing there," Mrs. Anderson said, "right in front of that window. The shades were up and she must have known I could see her from my dining room if I'd happened to be looking out of the window—not that I make a practice of looking into people's houses, because I don't. I haven't any desire to go sticking my nose into other people's business. But if a young woman leaves the shades up and engages in passionate lovemaking right in front of my eyes, she's got no complaint if I look. Land sakes! I'm not going to keep *my* shades down just because the neighbors haven't any modesty. These modern women don't know the meaning of the word. When I was a girl—"

"So the young man was making love to her, was he?" Mason prompted.

"Well," she said, drawing herself up primly, "in my time that wasn't what we'd have called it. *Love,* huh! I never saw two people carry on so in my life."

"But aren't you mistaken about the canary?" Mason asked.

"Certainly I'm not mistaken about him. Rita Swaine was holding that canary in her hand. She'd just started to clip his claws when this young man grabbed her in his arms. And the shameless way in which she twined herself around him made me blush for her. I never did see such carryings-on. She certainly never learned embraces like that in any young woman's finishing school. She just—"

"And what happened to the canary?"

"The canary was flying all around the place, frightened, and fluttering up against the windows."

"And the man had been there for some time then?"

"Yes. And he let her go and she was all flustered and nervous. She tried to catch the canary, and couldn't. The young man slipped out into the adjoining room. And then I heard the accident."

"So then you left the dining room window and ran to the front window, is that right?"

"Yes."

"And then what happened?"

She lowered her voice and said, "After this young man had gone back into the Prescott house, I went back to the dining room window. I couldn't help wondering what he and Mrs. Prescott—"

"Oh, was Mrs. Prescott there?"

"No, she wasn't," Stella Anderson said. "That was my mistake. I'd thought for a minute it was Mrs. Prescott, though. You see, Rita Swaine was wearing one of Rosalind Prescott's dresses. It's a print house dress that I know just as well as I know my own clothes, because I've seen it so often. She and her sister aren't twins, but they're as alike as two peas from the same pod. And, at the time, seeing that dress and not being able to see her face clearly, I thought it was Mrs. Prescott. And thinking what a pretty kettle of fish it would make if this young man *had* been that way with a married woman— Well, I'm glad he wasn't!"

"Perhaps it *was* Mrs. Prescott," Mason said.

"No, it wasn't. Afterwards I got a good look at her face."

"And it wasn't Mrs. Prescott?" Mason asked.

"No," she said in a voice which showed her disappointment, "it wasn't."

"You're certain?"

"Of course I'm certain. I'm just as certain as I am that I'm sitting here right this minute."

"You're talking now about something which took place after the accident?"

"You mean when I found out for certain it was the unmarried sister?"

"Yes."

"Well, by that time this young man had gone back into the Prescott house. He seemed frightened about something, and that's when he gave Rita Swaine the gun."

"A gun?"

"Yes— Oh, I wasn't going to tell you about that. Perhaps I shouldn't. You—"

"What kind of gun?"

"It was a blued-steel revolver. He took it from his hip pocket and gave it to Rita and she pulled out a drawer in that big desk near the corner of the solarium, and pushed the gun in back of the drawer and then closed the drawer."

"Then what happened?" Mason asked.

"Well," she said, "I'd already telephoned to the officers that there'd been an accident and that a man was hurt. I figured I could tell them about the gun when they came over here to question me. And then they didn't come."

"Was the man still in the coupe when you telephoned?"

"No. He'd been taken to the hospital."

"How long would you say it was after you telephoned that the officers came?"

"I don't think it could have been over five minutes. It *might* have been seven or eight minutes, but I think it was around five."

"And what did they do?"

"They looked the coupe over and took down the license numbers, and then this young man was just coming out of the house, and they took his name and address and looked at his driver's license, and then dismissed him, and then they got in their car and drove away without once coming over here. I can't understand it. *I* was the person that had called them. They didn't ask me what *I* knew about it."

"But, of course," Mason said, "you didn't see the accident."

"Well," she said, "I saw plenty of it. And, again, how did they know that? I might have seen the whole thing for all they knew. I might have been standing right there in the window."

"Yes," Mason said thoughtfully, "that's so. Whom have you told about this?"

"No one," she said, "except Mrs. Weyman."

"Mrs. Weyman?"

She nodded and said, "Yes, that's the next door neighbor over on Fourteenth Street. They've been there for six months now. Our back doors are just a few steps from each other. I told her about it right after the accident, within less than an hour. She's a wonderfully fine woman. It's certainly too bad about her husband."

"What's wrong with her husband?" the lawyer inquired.

"Drink!" she sniffed. "When he's sober he's all right, but when he's drunk he starts looking for trouble. He's always beating someone up or getting beat up. Land sakes, he came in while I was there telling about it. He was reeking of whiskey, staggering all over the place, and he'd been in an awful fight. Well, perhaps that'll be a lesson to him. He got the worst of this one."

"Did he admit it?" Mason asked, smiling.

"He didn't have to admit it. He'd had a bloody nose and a cut cheek and a couple of black eyes. It was bad enough so he'd had to go to a doctor and have his face bandaged. A pretty how-d'y-do when a man can leave a sweet, refined little woman like Mrs. Weyman sitting home crying her eyes out, while he makes a sodden nuisance of himself."

Mason nodded sympathetically.

"Getting back to what happened over in the Prescott house," he glanced casually out of the window and observed the square-shouldered, short-necked individual who was plodding his purposeful way toward the Anderson residence, "you say you had a good look at Rita Swaine—that is, you saw her clearly enough so you couldn't be mistaken?"

"Of course I did. Later on she caught the canary and came and stood right at the window. She seemed to want to get a lot of light on what she was doing. My Heavens, you'd think she'd been a surgeon doing a brain operation, the fuss she made over that bird's claws!"

"I'm wondering," Mason said, "whether you are good at remembering details."

"I think my powers of observation are quite normal, young man."

"Could you, for instance, tell me which foot she was clipping when she was so careful to get the light on her work?" Mason asked.

Mrs. Anderson pursed her lips, wrinkled her forehead into a frown, and then said positively, "The right one."

"You're certain?"

"Yes, I can see her right now in my mind's eye, standing there at the window, the canary held in her left hand, his feet up in the air—yes, it was the right foot she was working on."

"That was after the young man had left?"

"Oh, yes, that was after I'd come back from the Weymans'— Well, now, here's someone else coming! I wonder what *he* wants. Land sakes, this *has* been a day!"

Mason got to his feet and stood by his chair while Mrs.

Anderson, with quick, nervous strides, fluttered over toward the door. Sergeant Holcomb had hardly touched the bell button before she opened the door and said, "How do you do? What do *you* want?"

"You're Stella Anderson?"

"Yes."

"I'm Sergeant Holcomb, of the homicide squad. You reported having seen a young man over in the house next door hand a revolver to a woman who concealed it?"

"Why, yes," she said, "but I don't know how *you* found it out. I haven't told a soul except Mrs. Weyman, and a man who's calling on me—"

"What man?" Holcomb asked.

"A Mr. Mason."

Mason heard the pound of Sergeant Holcomb's feet, then the police sergeant stood scowling at him from the threshold. "So," he said, *"you're* here."

Mason nodded and said casually, "How are you, Sergeant? Better ditch the cigar. She doesn't want the curtains to smell of tobacco smoke."

Sergeant Holcomb made little jabbing motions with the cigar he was holding between the first two fingers of his right hand. "Never mind that," he said. "How do *you* fit in on *this* murder?"

"What murder?" Mason asked, raising his eyebrows.

Sergeant Holcomb said sarcastically, "Oh, sure, you wouldn't know anything about it, would you?"

"Not a thing," Mason told him.

"And I presume," Holcomb said with a sneer, "you just dropped in for a social chat, to ask Mrs. Anderson to go to a movie."

Mason said with dignity, "As a matter of fact, Sergeant, I called to investigate an automobile accident."

Holcomb turned toward Stella Anderson and raised inquiring eyes.

Her glittering eyes were fastened in beady indignation on the cigar which Sergeant Holcomb returned to his lips.

"That right?" Sergeant Holcomb mumbled past the moist end of the soggy cigar.

"Yes," she said, sniffing audibly.

"Okay," Holcomb said to Perry Mason. "You've found out about the automobile accident, and that's all *you're* concerned with. Don't let me detain you. I have business with Mrs. Anderson."

Mason, moving toward the door, smiled at Stella Anderson and said, "Thank you so much, Mrs. Anderson. It's a pleasure to meet a woman who sees and remembers things as clearly as you do. So many witnesses are putty in the hands of an officer who wants them to swear to facts which will support his theory of the case."

Holcomb cleared his throat ominously, but Perry Mason, smiling at Stella Anderson, slipped out of the door and walked rapidly across to Paul Drake's car.

The detective was seated behind the steering wheel.

"Find out anything at Weyman's?" Mason asked, sliding into the seat beside him.

Drake grinned and said, "I got thrown out on my ear."

"By the homicide squad?" Mason asked.

"No, by an irate husband. He's crocked to the eyebrows. Some guy's given him a beautiful licking. His face is patched, bandaged and bruised, and now he's looking for someone he *can* lick. The woman is nice. I don't think she knows very much about what happened, but this Anderson woman gave her an earful about seeing a girl named Swaine and some unidentified man hiding a gun. And Mrs. Weyman got to thinking it over and decided to call the cops."

Mason stared through the windshield in frowning concentration and said, "I don't like this thing, Paul. Why should a woman call up the cops just because she's heard that a next door neighbor and a boy-friend were hiding a gun? And why should the cops come out and start searching the house on a tip like that? Usually, you could phone things like that to headquarters until you were black in the face and get nothing more than a stall out of the desk sergeant."

Drake motioned toward the house and said, "Well,

there's your answer. Mrs. Weyman got more than a stall out of them."

"Tell me some more about her," Mason said.

"She's in the late thirties, rather slender, and sounds nice. She talks in a quiet, refined way, but there's a lot of determination about her. Her face shows unhappiness and character. Looking at her, you'd say she's been through some great tragedy and it had made her—oh, you know, sort of sweet and gentle and patient."

"Any idea what the tragedy was?" Mason asked.

Drake chuckled and said, "Take a look at her husband when you get a chance."

"What's he like, a big bully?"

"No. Medium sized. He's about her age, but he's an awful soak, probably all right when he's sober, but he isn't sober now. You know the kind I mean, Perry, four drinks and they're wonderful fellows, five and they're quarrelsome. And from then on they just get more quarrelsome. Well, I should judge he's had about fifteen drinks."

"What did *he* say to you?" Mason asked.

"He heard me talking, and came stumbling downstairs, busted into the room and made a scene. I could have hung one on his jaw and stuck around. But Mrs. Weyman was so embarrassed to think I'd seen him in that condition she wouldn't have told me anything more anyway. I'd already got most of it."

"Had the homicide squad been in there?"

"I don't think so."

"What did you tell her?"

"Told her I was investigating an automobile accident, and then asked her what was happening next door."

"She admitted calling the police?"

"Yeah."

"But she didn't say why she'd called them?"

"She said that Mrs. Anderson had told her about seeing a Miss Swaine, and some fellow who was evidently making pretty violent love to her, hiding a gun. And she said they looked guilty. She said that after worrying about it for some time she'd called the police."

"You didn't find out any more than that?"

"No, I didn't, Perry. I was just about that far in the interview when the trouble started, and I figured it was a good plan to get out."

"Well," Mason told him, "let's drive to a phone, put in a call for the office and see what's new. There's nothing we can do here while the homicide squad are making nuisances of themselves."

"Take both cars?" Drake asked.

Perry Mason nodded. "Let's clear out of the neighborhood," he said, reaching for the car door. "I'll meet you in the drug store on the boulevard."

By the time the lawyer arrived at the drug store, Drake was at the telephone. He scribbled something in his notebook and said, "Okay, hold the line a minute."

"I have a report on that accident stuff. Do you want it?" he asked Mason.

"Go ahead. Shoot," the lawyer told him.

"The Trader's Transfer Company, which owns the van, is a one-man concern. Harry Trader's the big shot. He was driving the van himself, delivering some stuff to Walter Prescott's garage. Prescott had given him a key. Trader says he was coming down the Alsace Avenue and was just getting ready to turn into Fourteenth Street when this chap, Packard, driving a light coupe, tried to pass him on the right without sounding the horn. Trader says he had to swing fairly wide to get the big van around the corner, and when he made the turn, the coupe was between the van and the curb, and it was just too bad for the coupe. Packard was unconscious, and Trader delivered him to the Good Samaritan Hospital. He stuck around there until the doctor told him Packard was okay, and could leave under his own power. He had a sock on the side of his head which had put him out. He was punch-groggy for a while after he came to. Trader says it was all Packard's fault, but he's fully covered by insurance and isn't going to worry about it very much. He said he was frightened at first because he thought the man was seriously injured, but that any damn fool who tries to pass a big moving van on the right, without using the horn and without watching the road, is a candidate for the boobyhatch. Trader says that after Packard recovered consciousness at the hospital, he admitted it was all his fault, said he wasn't watching the street, but was staring at something he'd seen in a window. First thing he knew, he saw this big van on his left, and then he struck it, just as Trader was making a right turn."

"Something he saw in a window?" Mason asked.

"That's what Trader reports."

"Didn't say *what* window?"

"Apparently not."

"Then it must have been either in Prescott's house or Stella Anderson's house. Let's run out to the hospital and see if we can chase down the doctor who treated Packard. I'd like to find out just what Packard said when he admitted liability."

Drake said, "Okay, Perry," turned to the telephone and said, "That's all, Mabel. Stay on the job and take down the dope as it comes in. The homicide squad's doing things out at Prescott's house. They're not passing out any information, but you'll probably hear details from one of the boys. As soon as you get anything definite, call me at the Good Samaritan Hospital. I'm going out there now. I'll call you again when I leave. Okay Mabel. G'by."

Drake hung up the receiver, turned to Mason and said, "Perry, I was just wondering. Do you suppose this Swaine girl would have any reason for wanting her sister out of the way?"

"Forget it," Mason told him. "If you *must* pin a murder on someone, hang it on the guy who was in there making love to the sister. Don't wish it off on one of my clients."

"Is the Swaine girl your client?" Drake asked as they walked toward the door of the drug store.

Mason said slowly, "Come to think of it, Paul, she isn't. She's the one who employed me, but I'm employed to represent the married sister."

"You mean Mrs. Prescott?"

"Yes."

Drake said, "Well, I'll bet you five to one your client's dead, then, Perry."

Mason said, "I think I'll leave my car here, Paul, and ride out with you. That'll give us a chance to talk. Just how do you figure it's Mrs. Prescott who's killed?"

"It's a cinch," Drake said. "According to Mrs. Anderson, the murder must have been right around noon, just before that automobile accident. Now, at that time of day, Walter Prescott, as a business man, would be at his office, but Mrs. Prescott would be playing housewife."

"Prescott may have slept late," Mason pointed out.

"No. Remember that he got Harry Trader to take some things up to his garage, and gave Trader a key to the garage. That shows that he was not only up this morning, but that he didn't intend to be home when Trader made the delivery, and Trader was coming to make the delivery just about the time the Swaine girl and her boy-friend were hiding the gun."

Mason nodded as Drake started the car. "Good reasoning, Drake," he said.

"It's a gift," Drake grinned.

"Then," Mason told him, "you might try this one: Rita Swaine and her boy-friend are at the *back* of the house, in the solarium, at the time of the accident. But Packard saw something in a window. *He* could only have seen the *front* of the house. Now, then, who else was in that house, and what or whom did Packard see in that window? And remember, Mister Wise-Guy, it must have been something interesting enough to send him crashing into a moving van."

Drake said ruefully, "You *would* bring that up. Okay, Perry, your clients have an alibi—if Packard saw what you think he saw in the front of the house—only don't forget it might not have been any crime at all, perhaps some woman who'd forgotten to pull down the shades—perhaps she'd got blood stains on her clothes when she killed someone, and was—"

Mason laughed. "There you go again! You have a criminal mind, Paul, and you'll be imagining my clients into the gallows before you're done. Step on it, and let's see what that medico says."

"Don't try crawfishing," Drake insisted. "*I* rather like that blood-stained clothes business myself."

CHAPTER FIVE

DR. JAMES WALLACE was still on duty at the Good Samaritan Hospital when Mason and Drake arrived. He listened to Mason's introduction with courteous attention.

"Indeed, yes," he said, shaking hands, "I remember the patient perfectly. He was received at twelve-ten this afternoon. For the most part, his injuries were cranial and superficial, but there was a most interesting condition which is sometimes encountered in cases of this sort. The man was suffering from traumatic amnesia."

"Translated into English," Drake said, "what is traumatic amnesia?"

The doctor favored Drake with a condescending smile and said, "Pardon. I didn't intend to use technical terminology. Amnesia is a loss of memory. Victims of amnesia know nothing of their past, cannot tell their names; of anything about themselves. And traumatic, of course, implies that the cause of the amnesia was superinduced by injury, that is, an external violence."

"Let's see if I understand you, Doctor," Mason said. "When Packard regained consciousness he had an impaired memory—is that right?"

"That's right," Dr. Wallace said in his well modulated, suavely courteous voice. "There were no broken bones. In fact, from what I hear of the accident, I would say he had escaped remarkably well. There were a few ecchymoses, one or two superficial cuts about the face, the possibility of a strained ligament, and, of course, the effect of shock. My treatment of his physical injuries took only a very few minutes.

"According to the statement of the man who brought him here, the collision had been rather severe. The patient had been unconscious when lifted into the truck. He regained consciousness as he was being carried on the stretcher to the surgery, but he had a complete lapse of memory. He couldn't tell us his name, his occupation, where he came from, whether he was married or single, or anything about himself. We searched his pockets and founds cards which showed that he was Carl Packard, of Altaville, California. I was very careful not to call his attention to these cards, or do anything which might refresh his recollection until after the effect of the shock had worn off somewhat, and I had satisfied myself there were no serious injuries. Then I gave him a brandy, talked with him for a few moments, and then quite casually asked him how things were in Altaville."

There was a moment of dramatic silence, while Dr. Wallace stood smiling at them, waiting for the effect of his strategy to sink in.

"Had I attached undue importance to the question," Dr. Wallace went on to explain, "the man would have sensed that I was placing too much emphasis on it, and unconsciously would have known why. Thereupon the temporary paralysis of the memory function would have been aggravated by a process of self-consciousness, just as we sometimes encounter in bad cases of stage-fright. We—"

"Never mind that," Mason interrupted. *"Did* he recover his memory?"

"Yes," Dr. Wallace said, the tone of his monosyllabic answer a rebuke to the lawyer's abruptness.

"Did he remember his name?"

"Yes."

"Did you have to tell him his name or did he remember it of his own accord?"

"He remembered it of his own accord," Dr. Wallace said with dignity. "If you will permit me to give you a complete report, I think you will get the picture a little more accurately."

"Go ahead," Mason said, pulling his cigarette case from his pocket. Drake looked around the room, sighed, dropped into a chair, propped his head back against the wall and closed his eyes.

"When I asked him how things were in Altaville," Dr. Wallace said, "I took particular pains to make my question casual. His answer was equally casual. I asked him if he knew the President of the First National Bank in Altaville, and he said he did, said he knew him quite well. We chatted along for a moment, and I asked him just where he lived in Altaville. He gave me an address which coincided with that on his driving license. I asked him his name. He told me. By degrees I brought him up to the accident, and then he remembered it perfectly."

"What did he say about it?"

"Said that he was the one who was at fault. The truck man, Mr. Trader, was very business-like. He said he was insured; that if he were to blame, the insurance company would pay, but he wasn't at fault. Packard seemed rather sheepish about it. He said he'd seen something in the window of one of the houses on his right, that he'd craned his neck to get a better look and then sensed something closing in on his left. The crash came almost at once, and that's all he remembers."

"Did he say what he saw in the window?"

"No, but he seemed a bit—well, embarrassed. I think 'sheepish' describes it."

"Was it a woman?" Drake asked, opening his eyes.

"He didn't say," Dr. Wallace remarked with dignity.

"Did Packard say what he planned to do in connection with moving the car?" Mason inquired.

"He said he was going out to take a look at it and see what could be salvaged."

"Is Packard insured?"

"I gathered that he was not."

"How long was he here?"

"Perhaps twenty minutes."

"When he left, he was all right, was he?"

"Oh, quite all right—that is, except for these superficial cuts and bruises."

"Did you," Mason asked, "get Packard's address?"

"Oh, yes. Just a moment and I'll get it."

Dr. Wallace consulted his file of card records, selected one, and read off an address, "1836 Robinson Avenue, Altaville, California."

"That's evidently his permanent address," Mason said. "Did you find where he was staying here in the city?"

"No, I didn't. I gathered that he was just passing through."

"Did you gather that impression from a direct statement made by him, or simply because of what you—"

"Certainly not," Dr. Wallace said, with dignity. "In my profession one does not rely upon inference except when it is absolutely necessary. I asked him when he had arrived here, and he said he had reached here this morning. That he had expected to be in San Diego by night."

"You didn't ask him where he'd stayed last night?"

"No, I didn't. I failed to see that that would assist me in any way in reaching a diagnosis, or prescribing a treatment. You must remember, gentlemen, that my interest in the matter is purely from a medical standpoint. Incidentally, I may say that it was a matter which called for rather delicate handling. To have impressed upon Packard that he was a victim of amnesia would have caused a sudden fright which would have been a cumulative shock, superimposed, as it would have been, upon the shock incident to the accident. You see, gentlemen, in a motor accident, there is not only the shock resulting from the injuries, but there is that momentary realization of impending disaster which comes a fraction of a second before the actual impact."

Mason nodded and said, "I understand. You haven't any more information which might be of value to me, have you?"

"None whatever," Dr. Wallace said, "other than that I may repeat, the man's injuries were not serious. Doubtless you are representing an insurance company which—"

"No," Mason said, "I'm not representing the insurance company. I'm interested, that's all. You have Harry Trader's address?"

"Yes. The Trader's Transfer Company, 1819 Center Street."

Mason said, "Thank you, Doctor. Come on, Paul, let's go."

Dr. Wallace followed them into the corridor, his manner suave, dignified and professional. "Good afternoon, gentlemen," he said.

As they left the hospital and crossed to the automobile, Drake said, in his slow drawl, "Where does that leave you, Perry?"

Mason said, "I don't know. I can't tell very much about it until after I find out what's happened at the Prescott residence. Right now I'm working pretty much in the dark."

Drake said, "Well, I'll call the office and get another earful."

"I'll wait here in the car," Mason said. "Tell your girl to run in to my office and tell Della to wait for me."

For some five minutes Mason reclined against the cushions of Drake's car, smoking thoughtfully, then he raised expectant eyes as Drake came running down the white stone steps of the big building. "Anything new?" he asked, as Drake opened the door of the car.

"I'll say! Plenty of news. The homicide squad was playing around the Prescott house because Walter Prescott was found dead in an upstairs bedroom. He was fully clothed for the street, and somebody had plugged him right through the brisket with a .38 caliber revolver. Three shots were fired. All of them took effect. One of them went through the heart. The shots must have been fired at close range, because there were powder burns on the clothing and skin. The cops searched the drawer in the desk where Mrs. Anderson had seen the Swaine girl planting the gun. They didn't find any gun in the drawer, but back of the drawer, where it had been shoved down into a little recess in the desk, they found a .38 caliber Smith & Wesson revolver, with three empty cartridges in the cylinder, and three loaded shells. The smell of the gun shows it had been recently fired."

"How about the Swaine girl?" Mason asked. "What are they doing about her?"

"They're looking for her. She left the house around two-thirty, carrying a suitcase and a caged canary. Police figure she intended to skip the country and didn't want to leave the canary in the house to starve."

"In that event," Mason pointed out, "she must have felt certain her sister, Rosalind Prescott, wasn't going to return."

"The police are looking for the sister, too."

"Any luck?"

"None so far."

"They've identified the man who was at the house?"

"Yes. A chap by the name of Driscoll. They're looking for him."

"Find him?"

"I don't think so. Not yet."

"Put a couple of men on the job digging out all the information you can about Driscoll," Mason ordered.

Drake's carp-like mouth twisted into a slow grin. "I saved a nickel on that one," he said.

"What do you mean?"

"I started a couple of operatives on him as soon as I had the name over the telephone, so I won't have to call back."

Mason nodded and said, "Get in, Paul. We're going to hunt up Harry Trader. We'll try his place of business first. He *may* be there."

Harry Trader, a barrel-chested individual, with the odor of stale perspiration and tobacco clinging to him, was still in his office, making out some reports. He surveyed his two visitors with cold, gray eyes.

"Just where do you two guys fit into this picture?" he asked.

"We're making an investigation," Mason told him.

Trader slipped a plug of tobacco from the pocket of his stained overalls, cut off a slice and inserted it in his mouth. With calm deliberation, he replaced the tobacco, shut the knife, and shoved it down deep in his pocket. "Yeah," he said. "When a guy starts asking questions, he's making an investigation. That don't mean anything. Are you representing Packard?"

"No, I'm not," Mason said. "I'm investigating another angle of the case."

"Which angle?"

Mason said, "An angle which is quite incidental."

Trader rolled the piece of tobacco about in his mouth through tightly clenched lips, and said, "Uh huh. Thanks for tellin' me."

"Did you take Packard to the hospital?" Mason asked.

"Yes."

"Did you take him out of the hospital?"

"No. I had a delivery to make. I turned him over to the doctor."

"You don't know when he left?"

"No."

"You don't know how seriously he was hurt?"

"Sure. He was just banged up a bit. I stuck around until I was sure there was nothing wrong with him."

"Was he suffering from amnesia—loss of memory?"

"He was punch-groggy, if that's what you mean."

"How did the accident happen?" Mason asked.

Trader adjusted the piece of tobacco between his molars, chewed with a barely perceptible motion, his facial muscles bunching into little knots as his jaws clamped shut. His eyes were cold and uncordial. On the wall, a clock clacked off the seconds.

"You're not going to answer that question?" Mason asked.

"You said it, buddy. I've made my report to my insurance company. Go talk with them if you want to."

"Just who is your insurance company?" Mason asked.

"That's something else again," Trader told him.

"Look here," Mason said, "for reasons which are none of your damned business, I'm trying to get this thing cleaned up in a way which will be satisfactory to all concerned. You haven't anything to lose by co-operating with me."

"You go see my insurance company," Trader said.

"But we don't know who your insurance company is," Drake pointed out.

"That's right, buddy," Trader said, "you don't."

"You were making a delivery out near the scene of the accident?" Mason inquired.

"Yes."

"To Prescott's house?"

"I don't see as it makes any difference," Trader said.

"It makes a difference as to whether you were really making a turn down Fourteenth Street," Mason pointed out.

"Yes," Trader said, "it was to Prescott's place. I had some stuff to put in his garage."

"And as soon as the accident occurred, you and some other man lifted Packard from the car and put him in your truck. You took him directly to the hospital, is that right?"

"That's right."

"Who was this other man?"

"I don't know. Some guy that came out of the house."

"What house?"

"Prescott's house."

"Do you know Prescott?"

"Yes."

"Know him well?"

"I've done some business for him."

"Know who this man was?"

"I've never seen him before."

"Would you know him if you saw him again?"

"Of course I would."

"And, when you found out Packard wasn't seriously injured, you left the hospital, returned to the scene of

the accident and made your delivery to Prescott's house—
is that right?"

"That's right."

"Was anyone home in Prescott's house?"

"I don't know. My instructions were to put the stuff
in the garage, and I put it in the garage."

"Who gave you those instructions?"

"Prescott. He gave me a key to the garage."

"When?"

"Ask Prescott."

"What were the articles?"

"Ask Prescott."

"When you made the delivery, the wrecked coupe was
still in front of the house?"

"Yes."

"Did Packard make any statement to you about where
he was staying in town, what his business was, or what his
plans were?"

Trader clamped his lips together again, and after a
moment puckered up the corners enough to send out
a thin stream of yellow liquid into the cuspidor which
stood by his table.

"Not answering that question?" Mason asked.

Trader shook his head. "He admitted it was his fault,"
he said at length. "That's all I'm telling you guys about
the talk I had with him."

Mason said, "Look here, Trader, you're not helping
us very much. I'm not trying to drum up a damage suit.
I'm trying to get information, and it isn't going to hurt
you any to give us that information."

"I've done all the talking I'm going to," Trader said.

Mason motioned to Paul Drake. "Come on, Paul," he
said, "let's go."

"Where to now?" the detective asked, as they crossed
the curb to his car.

"Take me out to my car," Mason said. "I'll drive it
back to the office. In the meantime, you start men finding
this chap, Carl Packard."

"How bad do you want him?" the detective asked.

"So bad it hurts, Paul. On all the other stuff we're tagging along behind. On this one thing, we're ahead of the police, or will be, if we can find Packard. What he saw in that window may save the life of an innocent man or woman."

"Or," Drake said dryly, switching on the headlights and starting the motor, *"may* hang a murder around the neck of your client. Have you thought of that, Perry?"

"No," the lawyer said, his face grim, "and what's more, I won't let myself think of it."

CHAPTER SIX

MASON fitted a latchkey to the exit door of his private office and entered, to find Della Street seated at her secretarial desk, telephoning. She said into the transmitter, "Okay, I'll tell him. He's coming in the door now," hung up, smiled and said to Mason, "Well, your lame canary seems to have brought you a mystery after all."

"I'll say. Who was on the line?"

"Drake's secretary. She said to tell you operatives hadn't been able to contact Jimmy Driscoll, Rita Swaine, or Rosalind Prescott. And, of course, the police are looking for all three, so they must have skipped out."

"All right," Mason said, "what did she tell you about the murder?"

"Nothing new. Prescott was found in the upstairs bedroom, shot three times with a .38 caliber revolver. The revolver the police found, where Rita Swaine had hidden it, was also a .38. Drake's men haven't been able to find out whether the rifling marks on the bullets are identical. The probabilities are the police haven't the information themselves yet. Tell me, Chief, if Rita had been mixed up in the killing, why didn't she say so frankly when she came in here? She must have known it would all come out. Having you working in the dark didn't help *her* any."

Mason crossed the room, sat on the corner of his desk and lit a cigarette. "Do you know what Paul Drake's men have discovered, Della?"

She nodded. "I was talking with Mabel Foss a few minutes ago. She gave me the latest."

"Then you've probably noticed that the only evidence which connects Rita Swaine with the actual murder is the testimony of Stella Anderson."

"Otherwise known as 'Mrs. Snoops,'" Della Street commented. "What about *her?*"

"It isn't about her," Mason said slowly, "it's about the evidence, Della. She says that Rita Swaine was clipping the canary's claws, that there was a passionate love scene between her and Jimmy Driscoll, that the canary escaped. And about that time there was this automobile accident. Jimmy ran out and helped load the victim into the van which took him to the hospital. Then Jimmy came back and gave Rita a gun which Rita hid. Then, as he was leaving the house, Jimmy ran right smack into the arms of the officers. Thereafter an interval elapsed during which the witness couldn't see what was going on in the house. Later on she saw Rita return, catch the canary, and finish trimming its claws. Now then, notice that, on *this* occasion Rita apparently needed plenty of light to determine what she was doing. Before, she'd been able to clip the canary's claws standing near the middle of the solarium, and without bothering to move the lace curtains. But when she finished the job, she found it necessary not only to come to the window, but to push aside the curtain and stand directly against the window, clipping the claws on the canary's *right* foot."

"But," Della Street said, frowning, "isn't that the foot that's clipped too closely?"

Mason nodded.

"Well," she said, "go ahead, Chief, tell me the rest of it."

"At the time," Mason went on, "Rita was wearing one

of Rosalind's dresses. Does that mean anything to you?"

Della Street shook her head, "Not a darn thing, Chief, except that I always felt I was short-changed by not having any sisters. Two sisters who are the same height and build can— Hey, wait a minute! You don't mean—" Her voice trailed away into silence as she stared at the lawyer with wide-open, startled eyes.

"That's exactly what I mean," Mason said, "Mrs. Snoops was standing in her window, looking in the solarium. She saw the frenzied love scene, and she saw Jimmy Driscoll hand *Rosalind* Prescott the gun. At the time, Rosalind and Jimmy were too engrossed in what they were doing to pay very much attention to their surroundings. Later on, Rosalind saw Mrs. Snoops standing outlined against the window, and realized she'd seen everything.

"Now, let's analyze that situation a bit: Rosalind was standing in the solarium in front of the desk, which is some eight or ten feet back from the windows. The windows are covered with thin lace curtains. It's possible to see through those curtains and into the solarium, but not too distinctly. On the other hand, Rosalind, standing there near the center of the room, looking *out* through those curtains, and across to the Anderson house could very plainly see the angular form of Stella Anderson standing at the window, very apparently an interested observer of what had been taking place."

"Then," Della Street said positively, "it *was* Rosalind Prescott Jimmy made love to and not Rita Swaine."

Mason said cautiously, "It looks like it."

"And was Rita in the house at the time?"

"Probably not," Mason said. "Remember that later on, when Rita appeared at the window with the canary, she was wearing one of Rosalind's dresses. It was a print dress with a distinctive flower design, striking enough in pattern and vivid enough in color so Stella Anderson could easily recognize it. She was more certain of the identity of the dress than of the person wearing it when she'd seen it earlier.

"Now then, let's suppose that sometime around noon Rita Swaine was summoned to the telephone, and heard the frantic voice of her sister saying, 'Listen, Rita, I'm in an awful jam. Jimmy Driscoll was over here and we just couldn't keep apart. He took me in his arms and I forgot everything and clung to him. Then I looked up, and who should we see watching us but old Mrs. Snoops. Now, you know what that means. Walter's going to sue me for divorce, and drag Jimmy into it if he can. We just can't let Mrs. Snoops testify that Jimmy was in the house, making love to me, while Walter was at the office.'

"Then it's possible Rita said, 'Well, lie out of it. Pretend that Jimmy's your brother. After all, *she* doesn't know who Jimmy is,' and Rosalind said, 'We can't do that because there was an automobile accident, and when Jimmy went to leave the house, the officers took his name and address from his driving license, so we're up against it. Now listen, Rita, I was clipping the canary's claws at the time. The canary got away and is still flying around the solarium. Jimmy has left, and I'm going to Reno. Now suppose you come over and put on that print dress of mine, which is the one I was wearing, catch the canary, go back over and stand in front of the window, as though you'd come back to finish clipping his claws. Make certain Mrs. Snoops sees you. When you see her looking, pull the curtain aside so she can get a good look. Then she'll see that it's you instead of me. That'll make her think it was you all along. Then you can announce to some of your intimate friends that Jimmy's madly in love with you, but you don't want me to know it right at present. Do it in such a way it gets back to Mrs. Snoops.' "

"Do you mean to say she'd let her sister in for that?" Della Street asked. "With Walter Prescott's body lying upstairs all the time?"

Mason shook his head and said, "That's exactly it, Della, I don't think she'd have done it *if* she'd known Walter's body was upstairs in the bedroom."

"But she *must* have known it if she went up there to pack her things."

"She didn't pack. She left that for Rita to do. And the body was in Walter's bedroom, not hers."

"Well, after Rita came to the house, *then* what happened?"

"That," Mason said, "is something else. Of course, Rita might or might not have gone into Walter's bedroom. Rosalind would have left the dress in *her* bedroom. Rita could have gone there and changed, then gone down and clipped the claws on the canary. Naturally, she was thinking more of registering with Mrs. Snoops than of what she was doing, so she clipped the right foot twice, without noticing that the right foot had been finished, while the left foot hadn't."

"One thing, Chief," Della Street said, as she stared at him through thought-slitted eyes: "Why do you say Rosalind Prescott said, 'I'm going to Reno'?"

Mason grinned and said, "That's a break. I went down to talk with Karl Helmold about the canary. Rita Swaine had told him I sent her, but she'd given him the name of Mildred Owens and the address as General Delivery, Reno. You see, Della, she intended to leave the canary there temporarily, but to send for him later on. Perhaps she knew that her name was going to be in the papers. Perhaps she'd already picked the alias of Mildred Owens and wanted to have it so the canary could be sent to her under her alias without any trouble, and whenever she wrote for it."

Della Street, staring at him, said, "And that means you're going to Reno?"

He nodded. "We're going."

"Going to try to beat the cops to it?"

Again he nodded, "And it may be dangerous, Della. We're playing with legal dynamite."

She scooped up a notebook, pencils, and said, "Okay. Let's go."

Mason helped her into her coat. "Naturally," he said, "it's important as the devil no one knows where we're going nor why we're going. We'll charter a special plane at the airport. Now, there's just a chance Sergeant Holcomb may start looking for me, find me gone, put two and two together, and take a chance on calling the airport. So you ring up and engage the plane under *your* name."

"Why not use an assumed name?"

"Because," he told her, "I don't want to do anything which would show a guilty intent. This is plenty warm right now. Before we get done with it, it's going to be *hot*. I don't want you to get your fingers burnt."

"Never mind my fingers," she told him, "but you keep in the clear, Chief. Remember, you're going to take a cruise around the world."

He nodded and said, "It'll be fun, Della, but I'll miss the action of a rough-and-tumble law business, at that."

"Don't worry," she told him, "you'll have plenty of action—dances on the deck in the moonlight, the beach at Waikiki, Japan in Cherry Blossom Time, across the Yellow Sea, up the Whang Poo to Shanghai, the Paris of the Orient, with—"

"You," he charged, leveling an accusing forefinger at her, "have been reading steamship literature."

"And how!" she admitted. "In case you want to know, Chief, I took all the papers out of your top drawer and loaded it up with pamphlets on Bali, the Orient, Honolulu, India, and—"

He circled her waist with his arm, swept her off her feet and around in a circle toward the door. "Come on, baggage," he told her, "there's work to be done."

CHAPTER SEVEN MYSTERY

CHAPTER SEVEN

THE MOTOR ceased its monotonous, rhythmic roar. The nose of the plane tilted sharply forward. Della Street, her face pressed against the window, said, "So that's Reno, eh?"

Mason nodded. Together they watched the lights as the plane banked into a sharp turn and slid downward through the darkness. The sound of the wind through the struts became audible as a high-pitched, whining note. The pilot flattened out, gunned the motor, and throttled down to a perfect threepoint landing. Then the motor roared once more into a crescendo of noise as the plane taxied up to the airport.

Della Street's face was glowing with excitement as she stood in the doorway of the enclosed fuselage, and Mason extended his hand. Wind, thrown back by the idling propeller, whipped her skirts closely about her. She placed her hand in Mason's and jumped lightly to the ground.

"Any clues, Chief," she asked, "or do we go it blind?"

"We go it blind. Get a cab," he told her. And to the pilot, "All right, get your ship fueled and ready to take off at a moment's notice. Get something to eat and hold yourself available, with everything ready."

In the taxicab, Mason said, "We'll cover the gambling places. I don't know about Rosalind, but Rita Swaine doesn't impress me as one who would stay in a hotel room —not in a city like Reno."

"What do we do when we locate her?" Della asked. "Try to shadow her?"

52

Mason shook his head and said, "We put it up to her, cold turkey."

"Suppose she tells us to go jump in the lake?"

"In that event," Mason said, "we'll get rough with her."

"How rough can you get, Chief?" Della asked, stealing a sidelong glance as she added demurely—"with a woman."

"Plenty," he told her. "You only see me on my good behavior."

The cab driver turned and said, "Where do you want to go?"

"The main stem," Mason told him.

"You mean Virginia Street?"

"Wherever the night life is thickest."

The cab driver said proudly, "There's life all over this city, brother, twenty-four hours a day. I'll drive down Virginia once, then turn around and come back, and you can pick the place you want to get out at."

Notwithstanding the lateness of the hour, the business district was crowded with people of various descriptions. Cowpunchers in high-heeled boots clump-clumped along the sidewalks. Men in shirt sleeves, without coats or neckties, rubbed elbows with men who might have served for fashion plates. An occasional couple in evening clothes sauntered from doorway to doorway, while women, evidently from ranches, went swinging past with the long, easy strides of those who live in the open.

The driver passed under the arched sign bearing the illuminated legend in blazing letters:

THE BIGGEST LITTLE CITY IN THE WORLD

"Okay," Mason told him, "drive back slowly. We'll get out on the other side of the railroad track."

The cab driver ventured a suggestion. "If you folks wanted to get a license," he said, "I could—"

Della Street laughed and shook her head. "Why speak of love," she asked, "when there's work to be done?"

She tucked her arm through Mason's, and, together, they walked a block to the left, turned to the right, and started making a survey of the bars and gambling houses. The third place they entered was The Bank Club. Here, faro, roulette, wheels of fortune, craps, and twenty-one furnished the main attraction to the Goddess of Chance, each having its little circle of devotees ringed by curious spectators.

Della Street clutched Mason's arm. "There she is!" she exclaimed.

"Where?" Mason asked.

"Over at the Wheel of Fortune. See her with that good-looking beige wool coat over the brown print dress?"

Mason nodded and said, "She's changed her clothes since she was in the office."

"Of course she has. She must have come up here by plane. That couple is with her."

"You mean the ones over on the left?"

"Yes."

Mason stood attentively watching the little knot of people who placed bets ranging from five cents to a dollar, while the wheel of fortune whirled its clattering course.

The woman next to Rita Swaine was chestnut-haired, brown-eyed, alert and vivacious. She was wearing a black dress with a frill of white at the throat, and a saucy, tight-fitting black hat. While Mason was watching her, she won a fifty-cent bet placed on the ten-dollar bill. The attendant slid ten, fifty-cent pieces across the glass top of the table. The young woman threw back her head and laughed.

"She's not wearing any rings," Mason observed speculatingly. "That may mean everything or nothing."

He shifted his eyes to the hatless young man who was with her, a man in the late twenties, slightly above the average height, with the broad shoulders, slim hips and easy grace of an athlete. Light glinted from his dark curly hair as his head moved. His eyes were black, smoldering with intense fires. The face was volatile and

animated. On the whole, a man who, once seen, would
be easily remembered, a man who would be quite capable
of gathering a woman into his arms, regardless of spectators, husbands or consequences. Della Street said, under
her breath, "And I'll bet he's a swell dancer."

Mason pushed past her, strode forward, and slid a sil-
ver dollar across the glass top so that it rested on the
twenty-for-one. Rita Swaine, without looking up, silently
moved over to give the newcomer room. The other young
woman raised frank, speculative eyes, swept Mason's face
in interested appraisal, turned to the man at her side,
and said something in an undertone. The wheel of fortune spun with a rapid whir which slowly resolved itself
into individual sounds as the stiff leather tongue beat a
fateful tattoo against the metal protuberances. Slowly, the
wheel came almost to a stop. The leather tab hesitated for
a moment, then, with one last faint slap, slid over into the
twenty-for-one subdivision.

It was inevitable that Rita Swaine should look up at
the man who had just won twenty dollars. It was as she
raised her eyes that Mason, scooping in his winnings,
said, "Are you going to introduce your friends?"

For a moment there was panic in Rita Swaine's eyes,
then she controlled herself, slid fifty cents over on the
twenty-for-one, said, "Just in case this should repeat—
Rossy, this is Perry Mason."

Mason half turned, to look down into brown eyes
which were no longer laughing, into a pleading, upturned
face. "I thought so," Rosalind Prescott said simply. "I
asked Jimmy if it wasn't."

"And Mr. Driscoll," Rita said.

Mason shook hands, felt the impact of the black eyes
on his, the long, firm fingers which circled his hand. The
face itself was as watchfully expressionless as that of the
gambler back of the faro deck.

"How did you do it?" Rita Swaine asked.

"It's a secret," Mason told her. "Where can we talk?"

"Rossy's room at the Riverside," Rita said. "—Oh,
there's Miss Street. Good evening, Miss Street."

Della smiled. Mason introduced her to Rosalind Prescott and Jimmy Driscoll. As though they had been casual tourists, sauntering from place to place in search of entertainment, they strolled out of The Bank Club and walked to the Riverside Hotel.

Mason dropped behind and said, "I'm sorry, Della, but you're not going up with us. This thing is loaded with dynamite. Stay here in the lobby and keep one of the house phones in your hands. If anyone comes in who looks like an officer, and who asks for Rita Swaine or Rosalind Prescott, get a call through to the room and tip me off."

She nodded.

"And don't let the others know what you're doing," he warned.

As they entered the lobby of the hotel, Della Street said, "Chief, if you'll pardon me, I'll run into the dining room and see if I can get a sandwich and a cup of coffee. I haven't eaten anything, and I'll have a terrific headache if I don't get something."

Mason nodded, said casually, "Okay, Della. Come up when you get through. What's your room number, Mrs. Prescott?"

"Three thirty-one."

"Let's go," the lawyer said.

It was Jimmy Driscoll who carefully closed and locked the bedroom door, after first making certain no one was loitering in the corridor. Then he opened his arms to Rita Swaine, and said, "Never mind, sweetheart, we'll see it through together."

Mason walked across the room, sat on the bed, flung an elbow over the brass rail at the foot, crossed his long legs and said casually, "You folks don't *need* to keep that up, you know."

"Keep what up?" Rita Swaine asked, spinning around to face him.

"That phony love act," Mason said, "Your sister might get jealous, Rita."

"What do you mean?" Rita Swaine demanded.

"You know what I mean," Mason told her, and then kept them waiting while he fished a cigarette case from his pocket, went through the motions of offering a cigarette to the others, selected one, sat back, lit it, and said, "After all, you know, I'm not Mrs. Snoops."

Driscoll said ominously, "I'm not certain that I like that crack, Mason."

Mason locked eyes with him. "No one asked you to, Driscoll."

"Well," Driscoll said, "suppose you explain—or apologize."

"Bosh!" Mason said. "What do you people think you're pulling?"

Rosalind Prescott, standing very straight, said, "*I* think Mr. Mason's right."

"Rossy!" Rita exclaimed.

Driscoll didn't take his eyes from the lawyer. "I don't think he's right," he said, "and I don't like his manner."

"You," Mason told him, "can go to the devil! I suppose because you're good-looking, women have been easy for you all your life. Now you're in a jam and you find it a lot easier to hide behind petticoats than to come out in the open."

Driscoll started for Mason. The lawyer raised himself ominously from the bed. Rosalind Prescott, jumping forward, grabbed Driscoll's arm, clung to it and said, "Jimmy, stop it! You hear me? Stop it!"

Mason said, "Go ahead, you young fool. Start something. That'll bring in the house detective, and then the cops. It'll be about on a par with the bonehead moves you've made so far."

Driscoll said with quivering lips, "I don't have to take this from you, you know."

"The hell you don't," Mason said easily, "You just *think* you don't. You'll take it and like it. Sit down!"

"Please, Jimmy," Rosalind Prescott pleaded.

Rita Swaine, staring across at the lawyer, said, "Why are you talking like that?"

"*You* should know. There are two reasons. One of

them is that I don't like to be double-crossed by clients."

"No one tried to double-cross you," she said.

"Oh, certainly not," Mason observed sarcastically. "When you told me that *you* were the one Mrs. Snoops saw with Jimmy, you weren't trying to play me for a sucker. You were just giving your imagination a few indoor calisthenics." He turned moodily to survey Rosalind Prescott and said, "I think *you'll* tell the truth."

"Shut up, Rossy," Driscoll warned in a low voice. "This is serious."

Mason appraised him with hostile eyes and said, "It'd be different if you could get away with it, but you can't get away with it. You didn't get away with it with me, and, in the long run, you won't get away with it with the district attorney. But, *trying* to get away with it is playing right into his hands. Why the devil didn't you folks tell *me* the truth in the first place, and let *me* tell you what to do? But no, you had to go on the amateur hour, and try and dress the window so it would look all nice and pretty. So Rosalind skips out and leaves her dress where Rita can put it on. Rita catches the canary, goes up to the window so as to make sure Mrs. Snoops can see her, and finishes clipping the canary's claws. Where she makes her mistake is in being too excited to notice that the claws on the right foot have already been clipped once. It's the left foot which was left unfinished. But Rita painstakingly cuts the right claws *twice,* and leaves one of the left claws untouched."

Rita Swaine said indignantly, "Why, I never—"

"You're right, Mr. Mason," Rosalind Prescott announced.

Mason shifted his eyes to her and said, "I think I'm going to like you. Tell me what happened, and tell it fast. We may not have much time. Your sister left a wide back trail. I followed it, and someone else may follow it."

Driscoll took a deep breath and started to say something. Mason said, "Shut up, Driscoll."

Rosalind Prescott said, "I fought with my husband.

He was going to divorce me. He found a letter Jimmy
had written. The letter was capable of two interpretations.
He chose the worst. He left the house to go see a lawyer.
I became panic-striken and did the worst possible thing.
I telephoned for Jimmy, to tell him what had happened,
and to tell him I was leaving. Then Jimmy got hot-
headed and came tearing out to the house. And, to cap
the climax, carried a gun, with some fanciful idea of
protecting me from Walter. Walter'd threatened to kill
me if I tried to claim any share of his business."

"You'd told Driscoll that?" Mason asked.

"Yes, over the telephone."

"Okay," Mason said, "remember it. Driscoll thought
you were in actual danger. You probably *were* in actual
danger. He carried a gun only for the purpose of protecting you. Now go ahead."

"Jimmy came out there. We were in the solarium. I
tried to talk things over sensibly with him. Jimmy—
well, Jimmy lost his head and took me in his arms, and
I—"

"Yes, I know," Mason said. "Mrs. Snoops described
the scene to me."

"How did it sound when she described it?"

"Passionate," Mason said tersely.

She met his eyes frankly and said, "All right, it was."
Mason nodded. "Good girl. Go ahead."

"Jimmy told me I must leave, and he was going to get
plane reservations. Then there was this automobile accident. Jimmy ran out and helped lift the man out of
the coupe and put him in the van. Then he came back,
and I suddenly realized he might be called as a witness;
that the man who was driving the van might come back
and try to get his name and address, and Jimmy's car
was standing outside, parked down on the side street. So
I told Jimmy he must leave at once, that I'd pack and go
later. Jimmy didn't want to go. I insisted. So then Jimmy
told me that I must take his gun, for protection, in case
Walter should come back. I told him I didn't want a
gun, and would never use one, but he insisted—I must

have one somewhere in the house where I could get it
if I had to. So I took the gun and hid it back of the
drawer in the desk, where I knew Walter would never
find it. I never did intend to use it, not even as a last
resort. I just took it in order to make Jimmy feel better
and so he'd quit arguing and get out of there. He's ob-
stinate at times—and this was one of the times."

"And then?" Mason asked.

"Then," she said, "I looked up and saw Mrs. Snoops
had been watching. Lord knows how long she'd been
watching—probably she'd seen everything. I told Jimmy
to leave. He started to go and ran into some officers
from a radio prowl car, who took his name and address
from his driving license. Then I knew we were sunk."

"Now, wait a minute," Mason said. "Did Jimmy come
back into the house *after* the officers took his name and
address?"

"Yes."

"And then what happened?"

"We talked things over, and Jimmy had the idea of
having Rita come over and put on my dress, catch the
canary, finish clipping his claws, and take occasion to
stand in the window where Mrs. Snoops could see her
and recognize her plainly. You see, we look enough alike
so Mrs. Snoops couldn't have been absolutely *certain,*
seeing through the lace curtains."

"Go ahead," Mason said.

"I rang up Rita. She knows the rest."

"Where did you ring her up from?"

"The house, but I didn't dare say much."

"How long were you there after you telephoned?"

"No time at all. Telephoning her was the last thing I
did in the house. I rushed to the airport, where I called
Rita again and told her everything."

"Did you come here in a regular plane, or a chartered
plane?"

"No, I flew to San Francisco, and then took a plane
to Reno."

Mason jerked his head toward Jimmy Driscoll and said, "How about you?"

"He came too," she said.

"On the same plane?"

Rosalind nodded.

"Now then," Mason asked, "when did you first know your husband had been murdered?"

Her eyes grew wide and round. "Walter?" she said. "Murdered?"

Mason, watching her narrowly, said, "Yes. Murdered."

"Watch out, Rosalind," Driscoll warned. "It's some sort of a trap. He hasn't been murdered, or we'd have heard of it."

Mason turned to stare at Rita Swaine. "You *knew* it, Rita," he charged.

She shook her head. "I don't know what you're talking about, unless it's some sort of a stall to get a big fee out of Rossy."

"Is that the truth?" Rosalind Prescott demanded. *"Has* he been murdered, or is this some sort of a trap?"

Mason continued to regard Rita Swaine with thoughtful eyes. "How did you come here?" he asked. "By regular plane or chartered plane?"

"I chartered a plane and came directly here."

"How soon after you left my office?"

"Within a very few minutes. I left the canary at the pet store I'd asked you about, then took a cab and went directly to the airport."

"And you didn't know Walter Prescott's body was lying in the upstairs bedroom of that house?"

"You mean Rosalind's house?"

"Yes."

She shook her head. "I didn't, and I don't think it was or is."

Rosalind Prescott abruptly sat down, stared wide-eyed at the lawyer.

"You didn't know it?" Mason asked her.

"No, of course not—it's—it's a shock to me. Not that I cared for him. I didn't. I hated him. You've no idea how cold-blooded, how scheming, how utterly petty he was! There wasn't a spark of affection in his make-up— Whether he's dead or alive, I *still* hate him—but this is a shock, just the same."

"Your husband," Mason said, "was found in his bedroom upstairs. He was fully clothed, ready for the street. He had been shot three times with a .38 caliber revolver. The police found the gun in back of the drawer in the desk where you'd hidden it, and they figure, so far, it's the fatal gun. If anything has turned up to change their opinion I haven't heard of it."

Mason turned to Jimmy Driscoll. "What was the gun you gave Rosalind?"

"A Smith & Wesson."

"What caliber?"

Driscoll hesitated, then said, "A .38—but that's not an unusual caliber."

"Any distinguishing marks on it?" Mason asked.

"What do you mean?"

"You know what I mean—anything by which that gun can be identified, any marks or scratches?"

"Yes. A little V-shaped piece was broken out of one of the pearl handles right near the butt of the gun."

"Was it blued-steel or nickel-plated?"

"Blued-steel."

Mason said in a voice devoid of expression, "Let's hear your side of this thing, Driscoll—no, wait a minute before you say anything. I'm Rosalind Prescott's lawyer. Probably I'm representing Rita Swaine too. I don't know about that. I'll have to figure it out. I'm *not* representing you, and I'm not going to represent you."

"I don't want you to," Driscoll said vehemently. "I have counsel of my own, in whom I have more confidence —a lawyer whose professional manner is far more dignified than yours."

Mason appraised him judicially. "Yes, you *would* fall for a dignified manner, proper clothes, a big mahogany desk, and the usual background of hokum. All right, that's settled. You have your lawyer. I'm Rosalind Prescott's lawyer. *Now,* do you want to say anything?"

"Of course I want to say something."

"Go ahead," Mason told him. "Say it."

"I want to corroborate Rosalind's statement in every way."

Mason stared at him with cold eyes. "Did you kill Walter Prescott?" he asked.

"Of course not. I didn't know anything about it."

"Did you see Walter Prescott while you were in the house?"

"No. I was with Rosalind all of the time."

"*All* of the time?" Mason asked.

"Yes."

"Every minute?"

"Yes."

"You're willing to swear to that?"

"Yes."

"Now, don't misunderstand me," Mason said. "You're going to swear that you were with Rosalind Prescott *every minute,* from the time you entered the house until you and Rosalind left together?"

"Yes."

"How about when you went out to lift the man out of the coupe, and when you met the officers? You weren't with her then."

Driscoll said, in a calm tone which just missed being patronizing, "That's while I was *out* of the house. I understood that your questions related to the time I was *in* the house."

"And all the time you were in the house, you were with Rosalind every minute of the time?"

"I've already answered that two or three times."

"Answer again, then. You were with her?"

"Yes."

Rosalind started to say something, but checked herself as Driscoll frowned at her.

"All right," Mason said, "then you were in the bedroom with her while she was changing her clothes."

Driscoll started to make some quick rejoinder, changed his mind, closed his lips on his unspoken words, glanced hastily at Rosalind and said, "Well, of course, she— How about it, Rosalind?"

Rosalind said, *"Of course* he wasn't with me while I was changing my clothes! He wasn't with me while I was packing my overnight bag. He's just trying to make an alibi for me."

"Just in case that's right," Mason said, "I wanted you to see what a price you'd have to pay for making that alibi. That question's going to come up. Either Jimmy Driscoll has to swear he was in the bedroom with you while you were changing your dress, or he's going to have to place you in that bedroom alone."

"But wait a minute," Rosalind said, "that was *after* Jimmy'd given me the gun. Mrs. Snoops will have to admit that."

Mason nodded. "Yes, you changed your clothes afterwards. But how about Walter, was his body lying in his bedroom at that time, or wasn't it?"

"Why—why, I don't know."

"How long since you'd been in his bedroom?"

"I hadn't been in all the morning. His bedroom is separated from mine by my dressing room and a bath. I met him that morning at breakfast. He was particularly offensive. He'd found a letter Jimmy had written me. He'd just been waiting for something like that. He'd taken twelve thousand dollars of my money, and I didn't have a thing to show for it. He was afraid I was going to demand it back and he was just looking for an opportunity to put me in the wrong and file suit for divorce, so it would look as though I'd thought up the money business after he'd filed and in order to save my own reputation by putting him in the wrong."

"I suppose you know," Mason told her, "this is going to sound like hell in front of a jury."

She nodded.

"According to Mrs. Snoops," Mason went on, "you

were trimming the claws of the canary when Driscoll came into the solarium and took you in his arms."

She nodded.

"Mrs. Snoops," Mason went on remorselessly, "had been watching you for several minutes before Driscoll came in. Driscoll wasn't in the solarium with you, but he'd already been in the house for some forty-five minutes. Mrs. Snoops saw him come in and noticed the time."

"She would!" Rosalind exclaimed bitterly.

"That," Mason said, "isn't the point. The point is, Driscoll wasn't in the solarium with you. Where was he?"

"Telephoning," Driscoll said quickly.

"To whom?"

"To my office. Rosalind's telephone call had caught me at my apartment. I dashed out to see her, and I had some orders which had to be executed first thing in the morning, so I telephoned my office."

"How long were you telephoning?"

"I don't know exactly, perhaps five minutes, perhaps ten minutes."

"And it was while he was telephoning," Mason asked, turning to Rosalind Prescott, "that you went into the solarium to clip the claws on the canary?"

"Yes."

"And prior to that time Driscoll hadn't gone in for affection?"

"He hadn't taken me in his arms, if that's what you mean."

"That's what I mean."

"No."

"So that's another period of time while Driscoll was in the house that you can't account for what *he* was doing?"

"No," she said, "I guess not."

"If you want to put it that way," Driscoll said hostilely.

"It's the way I want to put it," Mason remarked, without taking his eyes from Rosalind Prescott. "And it was while this telephone conversation was going on that the automobile accident took place outside?"

"Yes."

"And you let go of the canary and dashed to the front of the house?"

"No, wait a minute. I let go of the canary when Jimmy took me in his arms. Then Jimmy let me go, and I was all flustered, and Jimmy said he was going to call and make reservations for me on the next plane to Reno. So he went out to telephone, and I was getting ready to catch the canary, and then the accident took place."

"And, before that, Driscoll had been telephoning his office?"

"Yes, I believe so. It's all confused in my mind. I was pretty much upset by the quarrel with Walter, and then finding myself running away with Jimmy—well, I just can't remember things in detail. There are a lot of blurred impressions in my mind."

"But, all in all, Driscoll was at the telephone for several minutes, and on at least two occasions?"

"Yes."

"But you can't swear he was at the telephone?"

"No."

"What time did the accident happen?"

"I can tell you that. It was right at noon. The twelve o'clock whistles had just started to blow when I heard the crash."

"Then Driscoll went out, helped lift the unconscious man from the coupe, and returned to the house. By the time he returned you were back in the solarium, is that right?"

"Yes."

"When did you first know Mrs. Snoops was watching you?"

"After Jimmy had given me the gun."

"And that was when you decided that he was going to leave the house and you'd join him later?"

"Yes. I was going to the airport. He'd write me at Reno."

"And he went out, ran into the officers, had to give them his name and address, and then came back to tell you that the fat was in the fire and that you'd better let him go to Reno with you?"

"Not exactly like that. He told me what had happened. We realized it put us in an awful spot, so we sat down and tried to figure out some way of getting around it. Then Jimmy thought of having Rita come in and finish clipping the canary's claws where Mrs. Snoops could see her. She could put on my dress and go stand in the window."

Mason, looking across at Driscoll, said, "A clever idea —only rather tough on Rita."

Driscoll said, "At that time, Mr. Mason, you will kindly remember, I didn't know anyone had been murdered. I thought it was simply a question of saving Rosalind from having her name dragged through a lot of legal mud because of my impulsiveness and because I couldn't help showing my love."

Mason said disinterestedly, "Save it for the jury, Driscoll. They'll want to hear it more than I do. Now then, does either of you know what caused that automobile accident?"

Driscoll disdained to say anything, but Rosalind Prescott shook her head.

"I'll tell you what I've found out," Mason said. "Harry Trader, driving one of his big vans, was making a turn into Fourteenth Street, to deliver some stuff Walter Prescott had ordered him to put in the garage. He swung wide to make the turn. Packard, driving the coupe, came dashing up on the inside *without looking where he was going*. The first thing he knew, he sensed the van looming ahead of him and on his left. By that time, it was too late. The van was swinging in for the curb. Packard couldn't change the course of his car, and they struck. Now then, the reason Packard wasn't looking where he was going was because he'd seen something in a window of one of the houses on his right, which had arrested his attention. It couldn't have been the Anderson house, because Mrs. Anderson was the only one in that house and she was standing at her dining room window, look-

ing into your solarium. Therefore, it *must* have been
something which he saw in *your* house, Mrs. Prescott.
Now then, have you any idea of what that something
could have been?"

"None whatever," she said promptly.

"It *couldn't* have been in the Prescott house," Driscoll
said positively, "because Rosalind and I were alone in
the house. She was in the solarium and I was telephoning."

"That," Mason said moodily, "is what *you* say. What
do you suppose Packard will say when they find him?"

"I don't know and I don't care— What's the matter?
Can't they find him?"

Mason shook his head. "He wandered out of the hospital and disappeared. Now then, Driscoll, where were
you when Packard left the hospital?"

"What do you mean?"

"About an hour after the accident."

Rosalind laughed light-heartedly and said, "That's once
the breaks are with us, Mr. Mason. Jimmy was with me
at the airport—in fact, I guess we were already flying to
San Francisco."

Mason said, "Now here's something else: You people
are wanted by the police. *I* know you're wanted by the
police. Rita left a broad back trail because of that lame
canary. I traced her through that, and if I did, the police
may. Now then, if it were ever known that I talked with
you here and didn't turn you in to the police, knowing
that you were fugitives from justice, I might be held as
an accessory. The question is, can I trust you to keep your
mouths shut?"

Rita Swaine nodded and said, "Why, of course."

Rosalind Prescott said, "But we're not fugitives from
justice, Mr. Mason."

"Well, it looks like it. Why did you come here in such
unseemly haste?"

"I came here," she said, "because I wanted to get out
of the state so Walter couldn't serve any divorce papers
on me. I thought I could come to Reno and file a divorce
case of my own. After I got here, I found out I couldn't

do it until I'd had six weeks' residence. But I didn't want Walter to know where I was for a while because I was afraid he'd kill me. So this suited me all right."

"And Driscoll came here to be with you?"

"Yes."

"And why did *you* come here, Rita?"

"To bring some of the things Rossy needed."

"And you had to charter an airplane to do it?"

"Well," she said, "I wanted to tell Rossy that everything had worked like a charm; that I'd fooled Mrs. Snoops and that you'd agreed to represent her, and that she was to get in touch with you. I thought perhaps she could telephone you and arrange for an appointment. She could fly in and fly out and Walter wouldn't be any the wiser."

"You didn't go into that upstairs bedroom while you were in the house?" Mason asked.

"Not into Walter's bedroom, no. Rossy had left the dress on the bed in *her* room. I ran up to her room, changed into her dress, came down, caught the canary, put on an act for Mrs. Snoops, packed some things for Rossy, and took them with me when I left the house. I sent some other things by express."

"You had the express man call for them while you were there?"

"Yes."

"Where did you send them?"

"To Mildred Owens, General Delivery, Reno. You see, that's the name Rosalind had told me she'd register under, so I could keep in touch with her without anyone knowing."

"Sounds like rather an elaborate set of precautions just to avoid a husband," Mason pointed out.

"I can't help it. That's the truth."

Mason raised his eyes to Driscoll. "How about you, Driscoll, are you going to keep quiet about my having been here?"

Driscoll said, "You don't seem to have *any* confidence

in me, and I don't see why I should have any in you. I'll give you no promises."

"Jimmy!" Rosalind Prescott exclaimed. "Can't you see Mr. Mason is taking a big risk just in order to protect us? Can't you—"

The telephone rang. Mason pushed past Driscoll to jerk the receiver from its hook and say, "Hello!"

Della Street's excited voice said, "Sergeant Holcomb and two local deputies, with big *sombreros* and tanned faces, are just getting in the elevator, Chief."

"Grab a cab," he told her. "Beat it to the airport. Meet me there. If I don't show up in an hour, head back for the office. Hang up your phone, quick!"

Mason jiggled the hook up and down with his finger until the hotel operator said impatiently, "Yes, what is it? No need to have a fit! That hurts my ear."

Mason said, "I'm in a hurry. This is Perry Mason, a lawyer. I want to report that there are three persons in room three thirty-one who are wanted by the Los Angeles police. There's Rosalind Prescott, registered under the name of Mildred Owens, Jimmy—"

Jimmy Driscoll lunged for him. Mason, holding the receiver to his ear with his left hand, lashed out with his right, catching Driscoll on the point of the chin. As the young man staggered back, Mason went on evenly into the telephone, as though there had been no interruption, "Driscoll, both of whom are wanted for the murder of Walter Prescott in Los Angeles. There's also Rita Swaine, Rosalind Prescott's sister, who is wanted for questioning in connection with the same murder."

Driscoll, recovering his balance, came charging forward.

Mason slammed the receiver back on its hook and said, "Stop it, you fool! The jig's up. Now listen, Rosalind, you and Rita are going to be questioned. Don't answer questions. Don't waive extradition. Stand on your constitutional rights. Don't do anything unless I'm—"

A peremptory pounding on the door interrupted him. A man's voice said, "Open up in there!"

Driscoll stood glowering at Mason. Rosalind Prescott

was watching him with a puzzled question in her eyes. Mason pushed past Rita Swaine, and unlocked the door.

Sergeant Holcomb, accompanied by two bronzed men in Stetsons, pushed forward, then came to a surprised halt as he saw Perry Mason.

"You!" he said.

"In person," Mason assured him.

A grin suffused Holcomb's features as he said, "Well, *isn't* that nice. You knew that these people were wanted by the police. You smuggled them across the state line and—"

"Wait a minute," Mason interrupted. "I had nothing to do with their crossing the state line."

"That's what you say," Holcomb sneered.

"It's what I say," Mason said, "and it's what I can make stick."

"Okay. Anyway, we catch you here, plotting with them, avoiding the police."

"That wasn't what I was doing at all."

"Oh, yeah? Well, try and tell that to the Grievance Committee of the Bar Association."

Mason said, "As it happens I don't have to tell anything to the Grievance Committee of the Bar Association. I came here because I had reason to believe a person registered in this hotel as Mildred Owens was, in fact, Rosalind Prescott, who I happened to know is wanted by the police for murder. The fact that she happens to be my client in connection with another matter has nothing to do with it."

Holcomb said, "Try and make *that* stick."

"And," Mason went on, "as soon as I found out the true facts, I determined to surrender her to the police."

Holcomb said, "Don't make me laugh. My side hurts. I've heard some wild stories in my time, but that's the wildest."

Mason nodded toward the telephone. "If you'll kindly call the operator you'll find that I asked her to notify the police several minutes before you arrived."

Holcomb stared at Mason, said, "I'll just nail you to

the cross on that one before you have a chance to bribe
the telephone operator to commit perjury," picked up the
telephone receiver and said, "Did anyone from this room
try to call police headquarters?"

The receiver made squawking noises. Holcomb's face
showed chagrin as he listened. He said, "All right, forget it! The police are here," and slammed the receiver
into place. He glowered at Mason. "There's something
fishy about this. We'll pass it for the moment, but I'm not
done with it—not by a long ways. You're representing
Rosalind Prescott, Mason?"

"Yes."

"Representing Driscoll here?"

"No."

"Representing Rita Swaine?"

"Yes."

"All right. How about waiving extradition?"

"You're arresting them?"

"Yes. On suspicion of murder. Will you waive
extradition?"

Mason smiled at him and said, "I'll wave my hands,
and that's all."

"Get out!" Holcomb ordered.

Mason picked up his hat and said, "Remember, you
two, don't say a word in answer to any question unless
I'm there and advise you to answer that question. They
can't make you talk if you don't want to. Don't want
to. I'll do the talking. Don't waive extradition. Don't sign
anything. Don't volunteer any information and remember that they'll pull the old police gag of telling each
one of you the other has confessed and—"

The three converged on him, ominous purpose in their
eyes. Mason slipped adroitly into the corridor, said, "Good
night, *gentlemen,*" and slammed the door shut behind
him.

There was no sign of Della Street in the lobby. He
went by cab to the airport, found the pilot and said
"Have you seen anything of the young woman you brought
up here?"

"Why, no," the aviator said. "I thought she was with you."

Mason said, "Get your plane out and warm it up. Hold it in readiness."

It wasn't until the motors had been turning for several minutes that a shadowy figure emerged from the darkness to touch Mason lightly on the arm. "Everything okay, Chief?" she asked in a low voice.

"Lord, you gave me a fright!" he said. "I thought they'd nabbed you."

"No," she told him, "but I figured it would be a good move for me to keep out of sight in case they came out here prowling around. What did *you* do?"

"Covered myself with whitewash," he told her, "by telephoning for the police. Thanks to your tip, I had an opportunity to get the thing all planted before Holcomb pounded on the door. Holcomb's suspicious, but he can't prove anything."

The aviator said, "I'm ready. How about it?"

Mason nodded. "Let's go," he said.

CHAPTER EIGHT

MORNING SUN was streaming through the windows of Mason's private office, as he opened the door from the corridor and stood regarding Della Street with a whimsical smile.

She was standing by his desk, putting the finishing touches to an arrangement of maps and circulars which completely covered the top.

"Ship ahoy!" Mason called. "Where are we—Java, Singapore, or Japan? Lower the gangplank so I can come aboard."

She made motions of turning a windlass. "Okay, Chief,"

she said, "watch your step. Those sampans are tricky things to step out of. Here you are. Now climb this ladder. Okay. Here, give me a hand."

She stretched forth her right hand, clinging to the desk with her left. Mason gripped her hand, gave a long jump to reach her side and said, "How's this?"

"That's fine. Now you're aboard. What do you think of it?"

"Wonderful! Is this *my* steamer chair?" he asked, indicating the office chair.

"Yes," she said. "Just settle back and relax and look at the scenery. Over here's Honolulu. That's Diamond Head just beyond the beach at Waikiki. See the natives riding the surf with outrigger canoes? The circular says you get a speed of thirty or forty miles an hour, coming in for almost a mile, riding the crests of the huge breakers. Look at the way the water hissed up from the bow."

"Too tame," Mason told her, "I want to be the chap riding the surf board."

"They say that takes lots of practice."

"Well," he told her, "it'd be fun learning. Where do we go from here?"

She indicated the next circular. "Tokio," she said. "That is, the boat docks at Yokohama. We can see Yokohama and then take a run up to Tokio. And after that, here's Kobe," indicating another circular, "and then we cross the Yellow Sea and go up the river to Shanghai."

"How about side trips?" Mason asked. "Do we stop off in between boats?"

"We can if you want, but what you need is a rest. So I thought it would be better to get on a ship, pack our stuff in staterooms. Take all we want, and not have to bother with loading and unloading it, getting it through customs, and into hotels. In case you don't know it, you have a de luxe suite, all the way around the world. Starting Saturday afternoon you can unpack your trunks, put on your bathrobe and slippers, be where there are no telephones, hysterical women, or lame canaries."

"That's swell," Mason said, grinning. "Speaking of lame

canaries, do you suppose we could send a cablegram to Paul Drake and find out what's happening in the present case? After all, you know, we have to make a living in order to pay for de luxe suites on the Dollar Steamship Lines."

"Yes," she said, "I presume we *could* reach him by cable, although I hope you won't try to carry your business along with you."

"Oh, not in the least," he said, grinning. "Where are we now, in Kobe?"

"No. We were in Shanghai, the last stop. But, why bother with cablegrams? Why not use International Long Distance?"

"Now *there's* a thought," he said. "Let's get him on the line."

Della Street put through the call, said to Perry Mason, "Remember, you're only as far as Shanghai, then you go down to Hong Kong, Manila, Singapore— Oh, yes, that's one optional side trip. We can stop over at Singapore and run down to Bali, Java and Sumatra. I've arranged for that trip at your option."

"Okay," he told her, "let's take that trip. We may as well see it all while we're doing it. Besides, if we stay on one ship too long the captain might commit a murder and I'd have to represent him. Say, Della, how about stopping over in Honolulu, running down to Australia with Captain Johansen on the *Monterey*, and—"

She said into the telephone, "Hello, Mabel, this is Della. The boss is in and wants to talk with Paul. . . . Okay, put him on. . . . That folder up in the upper right-hand corner of the desk is the one on Bali, Chief. Better look at it. . . . Hello. . . . Just a minute, Paul. The boss wants to talk with you."

Mason whistled and said, "Wait a minute. Is *this* Bali?"

"That," she told him, "is Bali."

"All right," he told her, "we stop off at Bali. . . . Hello, Paul. What's new under the sun?"

"Read the papers?" Drake asked.

"Yes. I see that the police have taken a tumble to

Packard, and are giving plenty of publicity to his disappearance."

"Not only that," Drake said, "but they aren't getting anywhere. It's no wonder I couldn't locate him, with the limited resources which are available to a private detective agency. The police have been moving heaven and earth to find him and can't even get a trace of him."

"But surely," Mason said, "they must have been able to uncover something about him in Altaville."

"Not a trace," Drake said. "At any rate, nothing they can work on. Packard is the most important witness in this case, and he's wandering around the city somewhere, in a daze. The probabilities are his amnesia came back on him and he doesn't know who he is."

"You've been running down all the leads?"

"I'll say so. I've covered the hospitals, jails and every other lead I can think of. The police have been doing the same. They've combed the city, looking for an amnesia victim. They've uncovered drunks, idiots, crooks and bums, but not a trace of Packard."

"How about his coupe?"

"The police figure he might have contacted some garage to come and move the car, and perhaps given an incorrect address. I understand they've covered every garage which has a tow car and still haven't learned a thing."

"Have they moved the wreck?"

"No. They're leaving it there, hoping Packard may come back to it or send after it. If he shows up, they'll grab him."

Mason frowned thoughtfully at the telephone for several seconds, then said, "Come on in here, Paul. I have an idea I want to talk over with you."

He hung up the receiver and indicated his desk with a sweeping gesture. "I'm sorry, Della, vacation's over."

"You aren't going to stay in Shanghai?"

"No," he told her. "We'll have to let the boat sail without us, and come back on the clipper."

"That's what I was afraid of," she said, picking up the

folders one at a time. "Listen, Chief, you aren't going to back out on this vacation, are you?"

"No," he told her with a grin, "we sail, as per schedule, if I can clean up this case of the lame canary. And that case begins to look more and more complicated, and our sailing that much more uncertain."

Paul Drake tapped lightly on the panels of the corridor door, and Della Street let him in. Drake crossed over to slide into the big overstuffed leather chair, and said, "What's on your mind, Perry?"

"Simply this," Mason said. "That doctor out at the hospital was a little too self-satisfied, a little too positive, a little too definite in his diagnosis."

"What do you mean?"

"That traumatic amnesia business," Mason said. "The man had been in an accident. He had amnesia. Immediately the doctor decided it was *traumatic* amnesia. Nine hundred and ninety-nine times out of a thousand, it would have been. But then the patient wouldn't have left the hospital and had a return attack. Now then, Paul, suppose that it wasn't traumatic amnesia, but was a case of chronic amnesia? Suppose it was amnesia which leaves a man on the border-line of normalcy?"

"Is there an amnesia like that?"

"I don't know. I'm not trying to study medicine, I'm trying to list causes and get results. I want to add figures and get the answer.

"Now I've never had amnesia myself, but I've forgotten names that I wanted to remember lots of times, and I suppose a man who forgets his own identity has just about the same symptoms as someone who forgets the identity of another person. In other words, he has spells during which he can *almost* get it. The name does everything but pop into his mind, but vanishes again just as soon as he tries to concentrate on it."

"I know what you mean," Drake said. "Go on from there."

"If that's the case," Mason said, "this man Packard leads sort of an intermittent life. He wakes up in the

morning, or has a shock of some sort, and can't remember
who he is. He starts groping with the problem. He can
almost remember, but not quite. He thinks he's Carl
Packard of Altaville. He goes under that name for a while.
Then something happens and he forgets it. A man gently
reminds him of Altaville, and the association of ideas
brings the name Packard back to his mind. For a moment
he thinks he's Packard, but just as soon as the effect of
suggestion is withdrawn, he can't remember who he is."

Drake said, "What you mean is that the man's name
may be something like Packard, and he probably *does*
come from Altaville."

"That's it," Mason said. "Now, there aren't many names
which sound like Packard. But Packard is the name of
an automobile. Now, suppose you start men at work in
Altaville, looking up every person who has disappeared,
and particularly seeing if you can't locate someone by the
name of Ford or Lincoln, or Auburn, who is taking an
automobile trip somewhere and hasn't written to any of
his friends for several weeks."

Drake nodded and said, "It's a good hunch, anyway."

"Now here's another one," Mason said. "Let's suppose
this man has one of these spells, and there isn't some
doctor available to adroitly suggest to him that he really
is Carl Packard of Altaville. Then he'd be apt to take
some other name. Now, we don't know how long he's
been here in the city. So, in addition to the Altaville angle,
start men working on every disappearance which has been
reported within the last two months. In other words, if a
man walks out of a hotel or apartment and doesn't come
back, but leaves his things, under circumstances which
make it look as though he wasn't trying to beat a hotel
bill, we may have a live lead. I don't think it's going to be
very difficult to find those cases because the police will
have records of all of them. Get in touch with the Missing
Persons Bureau at headquarters, and sift through their
records. Do it in a rush, because the police may have
the same hunch, and I'd like to talk with Packard before
the district attorney sews him up. And don't forget Doctor

Wallace said he was headed for San Diego. So do some work on that angle, too."

Drake nodded and said, "I'll get at that right away. Now here's something else, Perry: I'm uncovering a lot of stuff about Prescott. Most of it doesn't have any particular significance and won't mean anything until I've got enough stuff to be able to put it all together in a complete report. But here's something *you* can get a lot easier than I can: Prescott had an account over at the Second Fidelity Savings & Loan. Naturally, they aren't passing out information to strangers about the accounts of their customers, but I did find this out: There's something fishy about it. Large deposits were made in the form of cash. And, unless Prescott's business was a gold mine, he was getting some cash from outside sources."

"Sure he was," Mason said grimly. "He got twelve thousand bucks out of his wife, and I only hope his account shows where he deposited that much in cash."

Drake said significantly, "If *my* information's correct, Perry, twelve thousand dollars isn't a drop in the bucket. He deposited over seventy-five thousand dollars since the first of the year."

"He did what?" Mason asked.

"Deposited over seventy-five thousand dollars. There's something over sixty thousand dollars in the account right now in the form of cash. Mind you, Perry, I'm doing a lot of guessing on this business; naturally, the bank isn't putting out any *official* information."

"You're all wet," Mason told him. "Whoever gave you the information has been making some bum guesses."

"Well, that's the way I figured it at first," Drake admitted, "but my information isn't so much a matter of guesswork as you might suppose. Now, here's my idea: You're representing his widow. She's entitled to letters of administration, if there isn't a will, or to be executrix if there is—unless, of course, the will specifically disinherits her. But, even so, some of this is community property. Now, suppose you go down to the bank, have a talk with them, put your cards on the table, and see if you can't get the information."

Mason said slowly, "They probably wouldn't turn loose with anything until after she'd actually been appointed."

"Don't be too sure," Drake said. "That's a nice, juicy account. They won't want to be too technical and antagonize the person who's going to inherit it, once they're satisfied that she *is* going to inherit it."

"Well," Mason said, "it's worth a try, anyway. I—"

The telephone on Della Street's desk rang. She picked up the receiver, listened for a moment, then turned to Perry Mason and said, "Don't let me interrupt, Chief, but Karl Helmold's on the line. He's so excited he can hardly talk. He wants to see you right away."

Mason nodded, picked up his desk phone and said, "All right, Karl. What is it?"

"*Ja! Ja!* Quick!" Helmold said explosively, and hung up the receiver.

Mason dropped his phone back into position, grinned across at the detective, and said, "Most cases hit you an awful wallop right in between the eyes with a mess of complicated circumstances which gradually simplify themselves when you start unraveling them. This case starts out with a lame canary and goes on from there in a big way. Every time we find a new thread, it makes the snarl that much worse."

Drake nodded. "One other thing, Perry: You could drop into the Doran Building and talk with George Wray, the surviving partner. Even if you can't get anywhere with the bank, you can certainly get places with Wray, because he'll have to account to the widow, and, as her attorney, you could make things rather disagreeable for him if you wanted to. You see, that's a partnership, and, as I understand it, on the death of one partner the surviving partner has to wind up the business. Is that right?"

Mason nodded, picked up his hat, grinned at Della Street and said, "I'm on my way, Della. That's what comes of hiring a high-class private detective to do the leg work. He drifts into the office with a lot of routine reports and sends *me* running errands around the city. I'm going to get shaved, then if anything urgent comes up and you want me, I'll either be at Prescott & Wray's offices in the Doran Building, or down at the Second Fidelity Savings & Loan. Come on, Paul, and walk as far as the elevator with me. There are a couple of questions I want to ask you. How about the gun the police found? Was it the weapon with which the murder was committed?"

"I'll say it was. Not only that, but they've tied it up to Driscoll by a manufacturer's number and a sales record. All three of the fatal bullets were discharged from that gun, and at close range. There were powder burns on the clothing and skin."

"What time did death occur?" Mason asked, holding the door open for the detective.

"The autopsy surgeon isn't too definite," Drake said. "You know how it is, Perry. They used to probe around in a guy's digestive apparatus, talk about *rigor mortis*, and give you a time as though they'd been standing by the side of the victim, holding a stop watch, when he croaked. Then that Thelma Todd case, and the Rattlesnake Murder case, and a couple of others hit them right where they lived, and they've been so cagey ever since they won't fix a definite time."

"I know," Mason told him, ringing for the elevator. "What's the best they can do in this case?"

"Between noon and two-thirty, and that's as far as they'll go."

"My God!" Mason exclaimed, "they found the body before five o'clock, didn't they?"

"Something like that, but between noon and two-thirty is the best you can get them to do. That suits the police all right, because it brings the earliest time limit just within the time Jimmy Driscoll was seen in the house with the gun."

Mason rang again mechanically for the elevator. His eyes were slitted in thought. "Wouldn't it," he said, "be a funny trick for Rita to play on her sister if—"

The elevator cage slid smoothly into position. The door

glided back and Mason said, "Okay, Paul, keep working
on those other angles. Get in touch with me if you find
out anything."

He was still frowning in thoughtful contemplation as he
entered Helmold's pet store. "Well, what is it?" he asked
of the excited proprietor.

"They took it, *Herr* Counselor. They took it!" Helmold
said excitedly.

"You mean the canary?"

"*Ja! Ja!* They came, the police, with many questions,
and they took the canary."

"Did they ask you about his being lame?"

"Not asked. But they looked at his feet."

"Did they seem to know anything about canaries?"

"Not them, but they talk of taking him to an expert."

Mason nodded and said, "Well, don't let it bother you,
Karl. It's just one of those things. I tried to get that canary
out of the way, but I couldn't do anything without involving you, and I didn't want to do that."

"It is evidence?" Helmold asked.

Mason nodded and said, "They think it is, anyway.
All right, Karl. Thanks a lot for telling me."

Mason dropped in at his barber shop and was shaved.
Then he called a cab, went to the Doran Building, saw
from the directory Prescott & Wray were in 382, took
the elevator to the third floor, walked down the corridor
to the inside offices, pushed open the entrance door, and
said to a red-headed girl who surveyed him with snappy
blue eyes, "I'm Perry Mason. I want to see George Wray.
Tell him it's important."

He watched her idly while her deft fingers flipped over
a telephone key, and heard her transmit the message. She
nodded toward a door marked "Private," and said, "Mr.
Wray said for you to come right in."

Before Mason had reached the door, it was pushed open
by a chunky man of forty, who clamped Mason's outstretched hand in a cordial grip and said, "Mr. Mason!
This indeed is a pleasure! I've heard a lot about you, read
a lot in the papers, but hardly expected to be so fortunate

as to meet you in the flesh. Come in! Come right in! Come in and sit down."

Mason turned to say over his shoulder to the red head at the desk, "If anyone should call, asking for Mr. Mason, will you see that I'm connected?"

Her eyes showed interest as she looked him over in frank appraisal. "Sure," she said.

Mason allowed Wray to pilot him to a chair. The automatic door check swung the door firmly shut.

"Well, well, I'm glad to see you," Wray said, assuming the conversational aggressive at once. "I'd thought some of coming to *your* office; but I realized how busy you were, and didn't want to intrude on you. This is a *most* unfortunate occurrence! Doubly unfortunate because Walter's wife is involved. I can't understand how the police could suspect her of anything like that."

"*You* don't?" Mason asked.

Wray shook his head vehemently. "Indeed not," he said with booming finality. "I've known her for eight or nine months. She's every inch a lady."

"You knew her before the marriage then?"

"Yes, I met her almost as soon as Walter did. They've been married about six months, going on to seven, I think."

"It was a brief courtship?"

Wray nodded and became suddenly noncommittal, his booming, genial manner obscured by a screen of cold, watchful caution.

Mason said, "Of course, under the circumstances, routine matters of administration will be delayed, but sooner or later, Mrs. Prescott will be entitled to some share of the estate, how much depends upon whether Walter Prescott left a will. I thought perhaps you'd like to talk things over informally in a preliminary way."

Wray regained his geniality immediately.

"Now listen, Mr. Mason, I'm only too glad to cooperate with you in any way. Mrs. Prescott won't be dependent on any will or any estate."

Mason offered Wray a cigarette, took one himself,

snapped a pocket lighter into flame and asked, "Why not?"

"Because it's all taken care of."

"How?"

"Walter took care of it. We have business insurance covering the death of a partner. His life is insured in my favor for twenty thousand dollars, my life is insured in his favor for twenty thousand dollars. The articles of partnership provide that in the event of the death of one of the partners, the wife of the deceased partner will receive the twenty thousand dollars in cash, in lieu of any interest in the partnership."

"Twenty thousand dollars, eh?" Mason asked.

Wray nodded.

"Rather a large amount, isn't it? If you liquidated your business, do you think it would run to a gross of forty thousand?"

"No, I don't," Wray admitted, and added with a grin, "In fact, I know damn well it wouldn't. That was the idea of making the insurance large enough so there couldn't be any question about it. In other words, the widow of the deceased partner would be tickled to death to take the cash instead of the half interest in the business. In that way, the survivor could keep the business going without having to wind it up. And then, of course, we paid the premiums on the insurance policies out of our partnership funds and those insurance policies were in the nature of a partnership asset which automatically increased our assets proportionately."

"And this was handled in a partnership agreement?"

"Yes."

"Did Mrs. Prescott sign that partnership agreement?"

"Oh, yes. She signed it, and my wife signed it. It's all drawn up legal and ship-shape. I'm surprised Mrs. Prescott didn't tell you about that. Probably she didn't fully understand it. And I presume she has plenty on *her* mind right now—tell me, do they actually have her in jail?"

"They're detaining her," Mason said.

"Well, it's a damn shame—perhaps she doesn't understand about this partnership agreement. You might explain

it to her. This insurance isn't part of the estate. The money
will come to me and I'll turn it over to Mrs. Prescott,
accepting from her her release as to any right in the partnership assets."

"Mind if I take a look at that agreement?" Mason asked.

"Not at all," Wray said. "In fact, I've been rather an-
ticipating you'd want to see it and have had Rosa dig
it out of the safe."

"Rosa the girl in the outer office?" Mason asked.

"Yes, Rosa Hendrix."

"Been with you long?"

"Not very—four or five months. Very efficient and very
attractive."

Mason nodded and unfolded the legal-backed document
which Wray handed him. After he had read it, he nodded
and said, "That seems to be well drawn."

"It is," Wray assured him. "Counsel for the insurance
company checked it over after our lawyer had drawn it."

Mason said, "As I understand it, when you executed
that agreement, you automatically froze the value of a
one-half interest in this partnership as twenty thousand
dollars. If the partnership assets were worth a great deal
less that that, the surviving widow would, nevertheless,
receive twenty thousand dollars. And if, on the other
hand, the partnership assets should increase in value, the
widow couldn't possibly receive more than twenty thousand dollars."

"We intended to take care of that by increasing the insurance in the event the partnership assets should show
any sudden increase," Wray explained.

"I see," Mason observed. "Would you mind giving me
an offhand estimate of the actual value of the partnership
assets?"

Wray lowered his eyes, to stare at the surface of the
desk for a few moments, then said, "Well, Mr. Mason,
that'd be pretty hard to do. You see, this is a personal effort
partnership. That is, we don't have assets of the kind you'd
have in a merchandising business, and—"

"I understand all that," Mason interrupted, "but what

I want to know is generally what would be a fair valuation of the partnership assets."

"Why, whatever our good will's worth."

"What's that worth?"

"Whatever we could count on taking in through our joint efforts."

"Perhaps," Mason told him, "I can get at it another way. Would you mind telling me how much you each took out of the business during the last year?"

Wray avoided Mason's eyes, swung from his office chair and started for the safe. Halfway there, he changed his mind, turned around, came back to the desk, sat down and said, "I think we took out about six thousand apiece."

"Each of you drew out six thousand dollars?"

"Around that, yes."

"Then," Mason said, "Walter Prescott couldn't have put any money *into* the business."

Wray suddenly smiled. His eyes met Mason's, and he said, "Oh, *that's* it. You're wondering about that twelve thousand dollars Rosalind Prescott said she gave Walter to put in the business."

Mason nodded.

Wray said, "To tell you the truth, Mr. Mason, she's all wet on that. She didn't put any money into *this* partnership."

"Do you think she gave him twelve thousand dollars?"

"Well, it's hard to say about that. If she says she did, then I'd be inclined to agree with her."

"And if Walter said she *hadn't* given him any money, would that change your views any?"

"That's rather a tough question."

"I know it is."

"Well," Wray said after a moment, "my answer stands."

"In that event," Mason asked, "what would Walter have done with the money?"

Wray laughed nervously. "Now you're asking me to be something of a clairvoyant."

"No," Mason told him, "I'm not asking you to do anything more than make a guess."

"I couldn't guess."

"How about women?"

"Oh, no," Wray hastily assured him. "No women. Walter wasn't that kind."

"What makes you think he wasn't?"

"You didn't know him personally?"

"No."

"Well," Wray said, "if you'd known him, you'd realize what I mean. He was sort of—oh, sort of cold-blooded—gave you the impression of having ice water in his veins —more the bookkeeping type. He didn't make friends readily and wasn't much of a mixer. I brought in most of the business. I like to circulate around. Walter—"

He was interrupted by the ringing of the telephone on his desk. Wray dove toward the receiver with an eager alacrity which showed he welcomed the interruption, said, "Hello," then nodded to Mason and said, "It's for you, Mr. Mason." He passed the telephone over, and Mason said, "Hello," heard Drake's voice saying, "Okay, Perry, you win."

"What do I win?" Mason asked.

"You win on hunches. I've done some fast work and located this Carl Packard under another name."

"What's the other name?" Mason asked.

"Jason Braun."

"Brown?" Mason asked.

"No," Drake said, "it's B-r-a-u-n, Jason Braun."

"Okay," Mason said, "what about Jason Braun?"

"He disappeared about two weeks ago, had an apartment on West Thirty-fifth Street, a bachelor place with maid service, rent paid up in advance, a few friends, a speaking acquaintance with the landlady, subscription to the daily newspaper, a couple of girl friends who occasionally dropped in for a cocktail, and the usual background a young salesman would have.

"Then he vanished from sight. Newspapers piled up in front of the door. The bed hadn't been slept in. Mail came and laid unclaimed in the box. A suit at the cleaners he'd been most anxious to have ready at a certain time

wasn't called for. One of the girl friends rang up the landlady, said he'd had a date with her and hadn't kept it.
She felt sure something must have happened to him. After
talking with her, the landlady notified the police. The
police found out that he'd taken his car from the garage,
as usual, and disappeared. He'd told the landlady he was a
salesman. No one seemed to know exactly what it was he
was selling. The police tried to check back on him and
came up against a blank wall. He wasn't registered as a
voter. They couldn't find where he was employed. The
theory of the police was that his employer would probably
make a report if it was a genuine disappearance. When
they didn't hear anything further, they just let the matter
drop. They have a complete file on the case at the Missing
Persons Bureau."

"How do you know that he's the man we want?" Mason
asked.

"Through the car," Drake said. "I went to the garage
where he kept his car, found he'd had some work done
on it recently, got the mechanic who did the work, took
him out to the wrecked car, showed it to him, and he
identified it absolutely, pointed out some of the work he'd
done on it. We're out there now. I'm telephoning from
that drug store."

"Any explanation of how this car happens to be
registered in the name of Carl Packard?"

"No, but it's Braun's car, all right, but the manufacturer's serial numbers on it don't agree with the serial
numbers on that registration certificate."

"You're sure?"

"Yes, the mechanic just pointed that out to me. When
he'd worked on the car it had different license plates on
it and had been registered to Jason Braun. The present
license numbers agree with the registration certificate to
Carl Packard, and the make and model of car is the same.
The rest of it is all haywire."

Mason frowned thoughtfully. "Well, Paul, we're getting
somewhere now. We can start tracing the registrations and

that other car should give us a lead. Keep working on it. I'll give you a ring after a while."

He hung up the telephone and said to Wray, "Well, getting back to this partnership business, I'm wondering if—"

"I beg your pardon," Wray interrupted, "but you mentioned the name of Jason Braun over the telephone. He's not in any trouble, is he?"

Mason kept expression from his face, picked up his cigarette from where he had laid it on the desk when he answered the telephone, and asked casually, "Know him?"

"Why, yes," Wray said. "I know him rather well."

"How long since you've seen him?" Mason inquired.

"Yesterday."

"Morning or afternoon?"

"Morning. Tell me, is anything wrong?"

"He was missing from his apartment," Mason said, "and his landlady notified the police."

Wray boomed into heavy laughter. "That," he proclaimed, "is a good one! Jason Braun missing! Good Lord, he's been right around town all the time. I've seen him two or three times during the past two weeks, and he was here in the office yesterday morning."

"What's his line?" Mason inquired, sitting back in the chair and crossing his long legs in front of him. Insurance?"

"Not exactly," Wray said.

Mason showed that he was waiting for Wray to answer the question in greater detail. The insurance adjuster fidgeted uneasily and said, "Well, after all, Mr. Mason, since you're representing Mrs. Prescott, I feel you're one of the family and I know I can trust your discretion. Braun represents the insurance underwriters."

"A salesman of some sort?" Mason asked.

"No, not a salesman. He investigates fires to determine whether they're of incendiary origin. If they are, he knows what to do. He's highly specialized."

"Something in the nature of a detective?" Mason inquired.

"Yes."

"What was his business with you yesterday?" Mason wanted to know.

"Oh, he didn't have any particular business," Wray said. "He dropped in for a social chat. As a matter of fact, he's my wife's cousin."

"Any idea where I could get in touch with him now?" Mason asked.

"Through the Board of Underwriters," Wray said. "But, look here, Mason, I'd a lot rather you didn't let them know I'd tipped you off to what he's doing. It's highly confidential, you know."

"The other insurance adjusters don't know about it?"

"Good Lord, no!"

"How about your partner, did he know about it?"

"No, he'd never met Braun. You see, Jason kept his identity pretty well masked because so many times he had to pose as a fire-bug in order to trap the people he was after. And, incidentally, that's why this business about his disappearance is a joke. I happen to know that right now he's working on a big case. There have been no less than twelve fires in the last six months which can be traced back to one gang of fire-bugs—no proof, you understand, but the underwriters are morally certain."

Mason said, "Look here, Wray, I'm going to ask you to do me a favor, something which will be of the greatest benefit to Mrs. Prescott. I want you to get in touch with Jason Braun for me. I want you to arrange for a confidential meeting at the earliest possible moment. I want to see him before he sees anyone else. Do you think you can do it?"

"Why, sure," Wray said. "Why, I can get Claire—that's the wife—to locate him within an hour."

"Remember," Mason said, "he left this apartment two weeks ago and hasn't been heard from since. He had an engagement with a girl friend and stood her up on that engagement. Confidentially, there's some evidence to indicate he may be suffering from an impaired memory. Circumstances which I won't discuss now indicate that—"

"Oh, I'm sure there's nothing like that," Wray said.

"He's working on a case, that's all. Claire will know about it. Why, I was talking with him myself yesterday morning and he was perfectly normal."

"He recognized you then?"

Wray said, "Of course he recognized me. My God, Mason, I don't know what you're after, but whatever it is, you're barking up the wrong tree. Jason's all right. Naturally, he's secretive in his methods, that's all."

"Well," Mason told him, "please don't misunderstand me. It's of absolutely vital importance that I talk with Jason Braun. I want to talk with him before the police do."

"The police?"

"Yes. He may be a witness either for or against Mrs. Prescott."

"Well, he won't be a witness *against* her," Wray said. "You can depend on that, because Jason Braun will tell the truth, and the truth won't hurt Rosalind Prescott. I don't know who killed Walter, but you can gamble *she* didn't. If Jason Braun knows anything, he'll tell the truth. No one can influence him one way or the other."

"And you think you can arrange for me to interview him before anyone else does?"

"I'm absolutely certain of it," Wray said.

Mason got to his feet, took out a card and said, "My telephone number's on the card. When you ring up, ask for Miss Street. That's my secretary. Tell her who you are and she'll put you on my line if I'm there, or if I'm out she'll see that your message gets to me and I'll call you back within a very few minutes."

Wray came around the desk to shake Mason's hand. "Tickled to death to do anything I can, Mr. Mason," he said. "And, incidentally, if Mrs. Prescott is in need of any cash to cover—well frankly, to cover her retainer to you, I can arrange to advance that cash. You see, the money will come in on that insurance policy within a few days and she'll be entitled to that. So I'd be only too glad to make an advance against it."

"I don't think that'll be necessary," Mason told him, "but it is particularly important that I locate Braun. If you can arrange for a confidential interview with him, both Mrs. Prescott and myself will keenly appreciate it."

Frederick Carpenter, first vice-president of the Second Fidelity Savings & Loan, turned watery blue eyes on Perry Mason, listened to the lawyer's statement of his errand with an expressionless countenance, cautiously rubbed the palm of his hand over his bald head and said, "I see no reason, Mr. Mason, why the bank should anticipate the legal procedure incident to probate. When Mrs. Prescott is appointed executrix or administratrix, she can file a certified copy of the letters of administration with us and we will then be very glad to turn over any money in Mr. Prescott's account."

"Will you tell me the amount of that money?"

"I see no reason for doing so."

"The court will have to take into consideration the amount of the estate in fixing bonds in the probate proceedings," Mason pointed out.

Carpenter nodded, stroked his bald spot with a cautious palm for two or three seconds and then said, "Of course, Mr. Mason, the circumstances in the present case are somewhat unusual."

"In what way?"

"Mrs. Prescott will probably be charged with the murder of her husband."

"That doesn't need to affect you in the least."

"I'd want an opinion from our attorney on that."

"How long would it take to get such an opinion?"

"I couldn't say."

"Look here," Mason said savagely, "I don't know how much money is here, but it may be rather a large amount. Sooner or later, Mrs. Prescott is going to have complete charge of that money. Your attitude isn't one to inspire her with any desire to co-operate with you after *she* gets in the saddle."

"I'm sorry," Carpenter said.

"That doesn't mean anything," Mason told him.

"I regret the circumstances," Carpenter amplified.

"And *that* doesn't mean a damn thing," Mason remarked.

"It's the best I can do."

"Well," Mason said angrily, "as attorney for Mrs. Prescott, I can tell you right now that your attitude isn't appreciated in the least. When Mrs. Prescott is appointed executrix or administratrix, as the case may be, you'll lose the account just as fast as she can check it out."

Carpenter observed blandly, "It's unfortunate."

Mason strode from the bank, his angry heels pounding the flagged floor. Behind him, Frederick Carpenter continued to stroke his bald spot with an even tempo of conservative caution. Then, as Mason passed through the swinging doors, Carpenter reached for the telephone on his desk.

Mason paused on his way to his office to telephone Paul Drake. "Listen," he told the detective, "I think you've uncovered something on that Jason Braun angle. I'm working on it from one angle, but that's no reason you shouldn't work on it from another. Confidentially, the man's an investigator for the Board of Fire Underwriters. He's working on a case right at present and his disappearance *may* have been deliberate, in which event that amnesia business *may* have been a stall. Now, the Board of Underwriters probably won't be anxious to give out any information, if they know why you want it. But if you can rig up a plant who will claim to have certain information about some incendiary fires which have been set within the last two or three months, the chances are the Board of Underwriters will send Jason Braun to call on him. Now, I want to get this angle covered before the police get wise to it, so get busy on it."

"Okay," Drake said.

"And one more thing," Mason told him, "get busy on a Rosa Hendrix who works at the office of Prescott & Wray. She's a readhead with a cat-swallowed-the-cream expression. See what makes her tick."

CHAPTER NINE

As PERRY MASON entered his office, Della Street motioned toward the door which led to the outer offices and said, "Abner Dimmick, of Dimmick, Gray & Peabody, and a young assistant by the name of Rodney Cuff are waiting for you."

Mason whistled.

"Why the whistle?" she inquired.

"Dimmick, Gray & Peabody are about the last word in legal aristocracy," he told her. "They're attorneys for some of the big banks. Their practice is mostly corporate and probate work. Now, what the devil do you suppose they want with me?"

"Perhaps it's nothing important," she said.

"Don't fool yourself," he told her. "Anytime Abner Dimmick makes a trip to my office, you can bet it's important."

"Do we show them in?"

"Right away," Mason said, "and with all the little flourishes and fanfare of trumpets royalty is supposed to command."

Halfway to the door, Della Street said, "You don't suppose they represent the bank do you, Chief?"

"You mean the Second Fidelity Savings & Loan?"

"Yes."

"Now that," he told her, "is a thought. Stay around and listen to what they have to say, Della. If I cough loudly, start taking notes of the conversation."

Della nodded, vanished through the door, to return in a matter of seconds, ushering in a white-haired man with

an acrimonious countenance, a heavy cane in his right
hand punctuating his steps as he walked. Slightly behind
him was a young man in the late twenties, in whose
china-blue eyes glittered a devil-may-care twinkle which
belied the self-effacing manner with which he kept a step
or two behind the older man.

The white-haired man in the lead pounded his way
across the office. "How d'ye do," he said explosively.
"You're Mason. I'm Dimmick—Dimmick, Gray & Peabody. Perhaps you've heard of us. I've heard of you."

He shifted his cane to his left hand, pushed forward his
right, said, "Careful now. Remember, I'm an old man.
I've got rheumatism in that hand. Don't try to crush my
bones. This is Cuff, Rodney Cuff, my assistant. In the
office with me. Don't know yet whether or not he's any
good. Isn't fitted for our type of work, anyway. We're
in a mess, a devil of a mess. Perhaps you've heard about
it."

Mason shook hands with Cuff, motioned his visitors to
chairs, and assured Dimmick he hadn't heard of it.

Dimmick clasped his interlocked fingers about the
head of the heavy cane, lowered himself gingerly into
the overstuffed leather chair. Cuff dropped into one of
the plain wooden chairs, crossed his legs, hooked an elbow
over the back of the chair, and gazed approvingly at Della
Street.

Abner Dimmick had a high forehead, fringed with gray
hair, bushy eyebrows which raised and lowered, punctuating his remarks. There were heavy pouches under
his eyes. His mouth was as decisive as the jaws of a steel
trap. A stubby mustache, matching the bushy eyebrows,
gave his face an appearance of frosty austerity.

"What's the matter?" Mason asked.

"Dimmick, Gray & Peabody mixed up in a criminal
case! Can you imagine it? Damnedest thing I ever heard
of!"

"You thought perhaps I could be of some help?" Mason
asked.

Dimmick nodded.

Rodney Cuff coughed disapprovingly. Dimmick flashed him a glance and said, "Go ahead, young man, cough your head off. I know what I'm doing."

Cuff lapsed into silence and lit a cigarette. Della Street let her amused eyes drift toward Perry Mason.

"We're counsel for Second Fidelity Savings & Loan," Dimmick said. "They're trustees under a probate trust. The sole beneficiary is a chap by the name of James Driscoll. Now then, do you get the picture?"

Mason settled back in his swivel chair, lit a cigarette and regarded his visitors with wary eyes. "I'm beginning," he said, "to get the sketch."

"All right," Dimmick went on. "Under the provisions of the probate trust we're to give Driscoll such legal advice as he needs. He isn't at liberty to employ any other counsel except with the permission of the trustee. Now then, he goes and gets himself mixed up in a murder case and there's hell to pay."

"Just why did you come to me?" Mason asked.

"We want you to help."

Again Rodney Cuff coughed.

"You mean you want me to act as attorney for James Driscoll?"

"Not exactly that," Dimmick said. "We want you to co-operate with us. We'll represent him. You're representing Rosalind Prescott. Their interests are identical and—"

"Pardon me for interrupting," Mason said, "but I'm not satisfied their interests are identical."

"Just as I was telling Mr. Dimmick," Rodney Cuff said eagerly. "It's very evident that—"

"Shut up, Rodney!" Dimmick said, without taking his eyes from Mason's face. "What makes you say their interests aren't identical, Mr. Mason?"

"Because I don't think they are."

"You mean you think Rosalind Prescott might have been guilty of some crime that James Driscoll isn't guilty of? That's impossible."

"No," Mason said, "I meant it the other way."

Dimmick said, "This is embarrassing to me personally, Mr. Mason. Very embarrassing. I never thought my name would be connected with a criminal case. But the bank insists I must supervise the defense personally. I can get some attorney who specializes in that sort of thing to sit in with me if I want, but under the terms of the trust I suppose I'm obligated to take personal charge. You can see where that leaves me."

Mason nodded.

"Now, then, *we're* willing to co-operate with *you*," Dimmick said insinuatingly.

Mason coughed loudly and Della Street, picking up a pen, casually slid around in her chair so that her right elbow was propped on the desk. Rodney Cuff said. "He signaled his secretary to take down what you're saying, Mr. Dimmick."

Dimmick shot his eyebrows down into a level line, shifted his eyes to glare ferociously at Della Street's poised pen, then turned back to Mason and said, "I don't give a damn if she does. Shut up, Rodney."

There was a moment of tense silence. Then Abner Dimmick wrapped his hands more tightly about the head of the cane and said, "The bank telephoned me you were down there asking questions."

Mason nodded.

"It might be a good plan to pool our information," Dimmick said, "to work out a joint plan of campaign."

"Thank you, I don't think I'd care to do that," Mason told him. "I want to be free to represent my client in whatever way seems best as the situation develops."

"Can't you see, Mr. Dimmick," Rodney Cuff said impatiently, "he's going to pin the whole thing on Driscoll if he has a chance."

Dimmick continued to stare steadily at Perry Mason. "I'm not very good at this sort of thing, Mr. Mason," he said. "I usually let the other man come to me. This time I'm coming to you. I know something of your skill in a courtroom. I know you'd be a valuable ally and a dan-

gerous enemy. Now, if you could see your way clear
to—"

"I'm sorry," Mason told him, "but I can't commit myself. I'm going to walk into that courtroom perfectly free
to do anything which seems expedient. I'm not going to
jeopardize the interests of my client by making any agreement with anyone."

Cuff said, "Do you mean by that, Mr. Mason, that
you're going to try to pin the murder on Driscoll?"

"If I think Driscoll's guilty, yes."

"Do you think he's guilty?"

"I don't know."

"If he's guilty, your client is guilty."

"Not necessarily," Mason said.

Abner Dimmick brought the head of the cane close to
the chair, pulled himself slowly to his feet. Rodney Cuff
said ominously, "Don't think we're going to sit back and
let you pin this thing on Driscoll, Mr. Mason."

"I don't," Mason told him.

Dimmick said irritably, "Well, I'll tell you frankly, I
don't like this sort of thing. I don't like courtrooms. I
don't like juries. I don't like criminal cases, and I'm too
old a dog to learn new tricks. But Rodney likes it.
Rodney's father's an old friend of mine. I promised him
I'd take the boy in. He doesn't like our practice. He's a
great admirer of yours, Mason. All he talks about is trying
cases, how things will look to a jury. All right, Rodney,
this is your chance to do your stuff."

Cuff drew himself up and said, "Please don't think I'm
completely inexperienced, Mr. Mason. I did quite a bit
of trial work in one of the outlying counties. My father
wanted me to get started in the city, and Mr. Dimmick
promised to take me on. I think you'll find I know my
way around in a courtroom."

"Glad to hear it," Mason said. "Glad to have met you
both."

Dimmick started stamping toward the doorway, paused
to wait for Rodney Cuff to open the door. "Well," he said,
"I don't like it. What's more, the doctor tells me I

mustn't get excited. Keep calm. Take it easy. Don't get angry. Don't get excited. That's what they tell me. Bah! Here I am, seventy-one, thrown into a criminal case, and if I get excited, it may kill me. Come on, Rodney. No need to take up more of Mason's time. Glad I met you, Mr. Mason. Good-by!"

He stormed out of the door, and the sound of his cane banging down the corridor was distinctly audible until he reached the elevator. Della Street looked at Perry Mason and burst out laughing. "Now *that*," she said, "is a situation."

"I'll tell the world it's a situation," Mason said, grinning, "and one not very much to my liking."

"Why didn't you agree to play ball with them?"

"Because I'm not going to tie myself up to Jimmy Driscoll—not until I know a lot more about where he fits into the picture. He shows too much natural aptitude to hide behind a woman's skirts to suit me."

"Emil Scanlon, the coroner, telephoned and left a message," she said. "The inquest is going to be held tonight at eight o'clock and Scanlon says he'll give you an opportunity to ask an occasional question if you want. He says as far as he's concerned, he's going to throw the whole case wide open."

Mason nodded thoughtfully.

"Won't that irritate the district attorney's office?" Della Street asked.

"Ordinarily it would," Mason told her, "but I have an idea the district attorney may be back of the move this time. He's in something of a spot. He must smell a rat, or he wouldn't have grabbed the canary as evidence. If Rosalind took the gun instead of Rita, he'd hate to charge Rita with murder. If the evidence gets mixed up, and he prosecutes the wrong person, he's going to have a hard time backing up and going after the right one. It would suit him just as well if we all started fighting."

"Then you're playing right into his hands?" she asked.

"Doing what?"

"Refusing to co-operate with Driscoll's attorneys?"

"That," he told her, "remains to be seen. I'm not going to let anyone tie my hands."

"Well," she said, "right now you have an appointment to go down and have your passport pictures taken. There's a Mr. Smith over in the Federal Building who was on one of your juries once. He'll rush through the application."

Mason nodded, grinned, and said, "Okay, Della, I'm going down to have my picture taken and get my passport."

"I'll let you see my passport picture if you'll let me see yours," she promised.

"Maybe we should get enlargements and hang 'em side by side in the office so the clients could have a treat," Mason suggested.

She shook her head. "You know how passport pictures are. We'd look like a couple of crooks."

Mason paused with his hand on the knob of the door and grinned across at her. "Well," he asked, "aren't we?"

CHAPTER TEN

THE RESPONSIBILITIES of his office rested lightly on the shoulders of Emil Scanlon, the coroner. Tall, middle-aged, good-natured, he regarded the gruesome aftermaths of tragedies which flowed through his office with the detached interest of a scientist viewing guinea pigs. He was a sympathetic man, but he reserved his sympathies for the living, where they could do some good, rather than for the mangled remains upon which he was so frequently called to hold inquest.

He called the inquest to order in a good-natured, matter-of-fact voice, his keen eyes flitting over the crowded room.

"The jury has now viewed the remains," he said, "and we're ready to take testimony. The proceedings here are going to be informal. In other words, I'm not going to stand on a lot of technicalities. Apparently this man didn't commit suicide. Three people are being held by the authorities. They're Rosalind Prescott, the widow, Rita Swaine, the decedent's sister-in-law, and James Driscoll. Driscoll waived extradition and is here. Miss Swaine and the widow refused to waive extradition and are not here, so we can't call them as witnesses. Oscar Overmeyer, the deputy district attorney, is representing the interests of The People. Perry Mason is representing Miss Swaine and Mrs. Prescott, and Rodney Cuff is representing Mr. Driscoll. Now, obviously, if these attorneys start getting technical and are allowed to get away with it, we'll be here all night. The idea of this inquest isn't to prove anybody guilty beyond all reasonable doubt, it's simply to ascertain how the decedent met his death. In other words, we want to know just what caused Walter Prescott to die. And if the probabilities are someone killed him, we want to know who that someone was.

"Now, I'm to go ahead with this inquest, and if any of the interested parties want to co-operate with me, I'll be glad to have them. But I'm not going to have this inquest used as an excuse to mix things up. Do you gentlemen understand me?"

The three attorneys nodded.

"The first witness," Scanlon said, "will be George Wray."

Wray held up his hand and was sworn.

"You've seen the remains of the decedent?" Scanlon asked.

"Yes."

"Can you identify them?"

"Absolutely. Those are the remains of Walter Prescott, who was my partner in the firm of Prescott & Wray."

"What sort of business?" Scanlon asked.

"Insurance adjusting."

"When did you last see him alive?"

"The day before yesterday."

"Did you talk with him yesterday?"

"Yes."

"Over the telephone?"

"That's right."

"At what time?"

"At approximately five minutes to twelve. I happened to look at the clock at the time."

"Did he say where he was?"

"No, he didn't. He said he expected to arrive at the office during the first part of the afternoon, and I happened to notice the time when he was telephoning because I'd had rather a busy morning and had more or less lost track of time."

"What time was it?"

"Almost exactly five minutes of twelve. I think it was about five and one-half minutes."

"By an office clock?"

"Yes."

"You've checked that office clock since?"

"Yes, it's an electric clock. It's absolutely right to the second."

"That's all," the coroner said.

"May I ask one question?" Perry Mason inquired.

The coroner nodded his permission, and Mason said, "Did you go out to lunch shortly after that telephone conversation, Mr. Wray?"

"Immediately afterwards," Wray said.

"That's all, thank you."

Dr. Hubert, an autopsy surgeon, was called, identified three bullets, one of which had been taken from the body of the deceased, the remaining pair having been found in the room after having evidently passed entirely through the decedent's body.

The physician described the course of the bullets. One of them had inflicted a wound which would not necessarily have been fatal. The other two inflicted wounds which were instantaneously fatal. Powder marks indicated the shots had been fired at close range. He described how the body had been found, and testified that death had been instantaneous. He fixed the time of death as between noon and two-thirty in the afternoon. The body had been discovered shortly before five o'clock in the evening.

E. Q. James, a criminologist attached to the district attorney's office, identified a gun, together with microphotographs of test bullets which had been fired from that gun which showed that they were identical with the three bullets which had been placed in evidence by the autopsy surgeon.

The coroner called Stella Anderson. She strode up to the witness stand, back rigid, chin up, eyes flashing, her flushed face showing her enjoyment at finding herself in the limelight. While she testified as to her name and residence, newspaper photographers snapped flashlight photographs of her on the witness stand.

Under questioning by the coroner, she repeated what she had seen in the Prescott house the previous day.

"And you saw this young man give the young woman a gun?" Scanlon asked.

"Yes, sir, I saw him hand her a gun. She opened the drawer in the desk and pushed it down in behind the drawer, then closed the drawer."

"Who was this man?"

"That man sitting right there. The one in the blue suit."

"You mean James Driscoll? . . . Stand up, Mr. James Driscoll. . . . Is that the man, Mrs. Anderson?"

"Yes—that is, he's the man I saw running out of the Prescott house right after the accident, and he *looks* just like the man I saw with the gun. You see, those windows have very thin lace curtains behind them, and you can't see quite as clearly as if they weren't there. Not *quite,* but pretty near. I'm pretty positive that man I saw with the gun was this young man, James Driscoll."

"Now, who was this woman?"

She faced him frankly and said, "I don't know. I *thought* it was Rosalind Prescott. But later on, Rita Swaine appeared at the window wearing exactly that same dress, and trying to make me think—"

"Never mind what she tried to make you think," the coroner said. "Just tell what you saw."

Mrs. Anderson pressed her lips tightly together and said, "Well, I have my own opinion."

There was a titter in the room, which was silenced by the coroner's gavel. "Just what did you *see*, Mrs. Anderson?" he asked.

"I saw Rita Swaine standing at the window and clipping the canary's claws."

"Which foot, the right or the left?"

"The right."

The coroner thanked her, excused her from the stand, and nodded toward Driscoll, who sat between a deputy sheriff on one side and Rodney Cuff on the other.

"Mr. Driscoll," the coroner said, "as a matter of form, I'm going to ask you to take the stand and answer some questions. I realize, of course, that your attorney won't allow you to answer them, but, just for the sake of keeping the record clear, I want your refusal to answer my questions to appear in the record of this inquest."

Rodney Cuff, on his feet, was smiling and urbane. His voice, seemingly elevated hardly above a conversational tone, filled the crowded room with a vibrant resonance. "I think," he said, "your Honor misunderstands our position. It is only the guilty who need to take refuge in technicalities. So far as James Driscoll is concerned, he will unhesitatingly answer any question put to him by the coroner or the deputy district attorney."

There was a ripple of audible surprise in the room. Emil Scanlon exchanged puzzled glances with the deputy district attorney, then swore Driscoll as a witness.

"You're acquainted with the decedent, Mr. Driscoll?" the coroner asked.

"Yes, I'd seen him once or twice."

"You were acquainted with Mrs. Prescott?"

"Yes."

"How long had you known her?"

"Something over eighteen months."

"Had you at one time been engaged to her?"

"Yes."

"What happened to that engagement?"

Driscoll moistened his lips with his tongue and said, "It was broken because of a quarrel."

"How soon after that did she marry the decedent?"

"Within a month."

"Now then, Mr. Driscoll, I'll ask you if a letter was written by you and sent to Mrs. Prescott in which you suggested she leave her husband and get a divorce."

"The letter itself is the best evidence," Mason objected.

Cuff smiled. "I understand Mr. Mason's objection perfectly," he said. "But questions and answers will never incriminate this witness because he's completely innocent. Go right ahead and answer the question, Jimmy."

Driscoll said, "I wrote such a letter, signed it, put it in a stamped, addressed envelope, and mailed it to Mrs. Prescott. That was, I believe, four or five days ago."

"In this letter you advised Mrs. Prescott to leave her husband?" the coroner asked.

"Yes."

"You didn't feel friendly toward him?"

"I did not. I thought he was a crook and a cheat."

"You were jealous of him?"

"In a way, yes."

"You had reason to hate him?"

"Frankly, I did."

The coroner glanced appealingly at Cuff, then over to the deputy district attorney, and said, "I've never heard anything quite like this."

Overmeyer nodded. Rodney Cuff said cordially, "Go right ahead, your Honor. You're doing fine. Or would you prefer to have me ask the questions?"

"No," the coroner said, "I'll ask them. Now, you were in Walter Prescott's house yesterday morning, Mr. Driscoll?"

"Yes."

"At about what time?"

"At about the time mentioned by Mrs. Anderson. I

didn't look at my watch, but it was just a few minutes after eleven when I arrived."

"Did Walter Prescott know you were coming?"

"No."

"Had he invited you to visit his house?"

"No."

"You went there for the purpose of seeing his wife?"

"Yes."

"You saw her?"

"Yes."

"And you armed yourself before going to the house?"

"I did. Walter Prescott had threatened to kill her. I considered him fully capable of doing just that. I intended to protect her from him."

"By using that weapon?"

"I didn't think *I'd* need to use it, but I wanted her to have it so she could use it if she had to in order to defend herself."

"Did you make any protestations of love or affection to Mrs. Prescott?"

"I did," Driscoll said, with some feeling. "I couldn't bear the thought of her being unhappy. My emotions got the best of me. I took her in my arms and told her I still loved her; that I had always loved her."

He was leaning slightly forward in the chair now, breathing rapidly. Press photographers pushed forward. Cameras clicked audibly.

The coroner said, "Let's not have any misunderstanding about this, Mr. Driscoll. Did you kill Walter Prescott?"

"I did not."

"Did you know he was dead?"

"Not until long after I had left the house."

"Will you describe just what you did in the house after, let us say, eleven-thirty?"

"I was talking with Mrs. Prescott about her financial affairs and the embezzlement of some twelve thousand dollars of her money by her husband. He had deliberately manipulated her affairs so he could steal this money."

"Do I understand you communicated these sentiments to Walter Prescott's wife?"

"Exactly," Driscoll said with feeling. "He'd swindled her, lied to her and cheated her. He only married her for her money. I felt that he'd forfeited any rights he might have had as a husband."

"But you knew the law regarded him as her legal husband and still clothed him with the rights of a husband?"

"Yes."

"You knew there'd been no suit for divorce filed?"

"Yes."

"And yet, before you left that house, you were planning to run away with this woman?"

"I was planning to take her to Reno, where she could institute a divorce action. At first I intended to let her go by herself. Later on I decided to join her on her trip."

"And you did so?"

"I did."

"Did you know Walter Prescott was dead when you left the house?"

"I did not."

"Let's get back now to what you were doing after eleven-thirty."

"I lost my self-control and took Mrs. Prescott in my arms and told her that I loved her. Mrs. Anderson, watching from the adjoining house, can bear witness to that."

Stella Anderson nodded vigorously.

The coroner said, "Never mind, Mrs. Anderson. You're not on the witness stand now. You've already given your testimony. Go ahead, Mr. Driscoll. Tell us what happened after that."

"After that I stepped into the other room to telephone the airport to get a reservation on the plane for Mrs. Prescott. I had just about finished telephoning when an automobile accident occurred in front of the place. I ran out to render what assistance I could, and then returned. Knowing that, because of the accident, I might be subpoenaed at any moment as a witness to that accident, and not wishing to leave Rosalind Prescott unprotected, I took the revolver from my pocket and gave it to her. That's the Smith & Wesson .38 caliber revolver which has been introduced in evidence here. It was my revolver, but at the time I gave it to Mrs. Prescott it had not been fired. She told me that her husband had threatened to take her life, and I wanted her to have some means of protecting herself."

"Then what did you do?"

"Then I left the house and ran into a couple of radio officers. They took my name, license number, and address, and told me I might be a witness. I told them I'd been telephoning at the time and hadn't seen anything of what had occurred, but that didn't seem to make any difference with them. Then I returned to Prescott's house, told Rosalind Prescott that my identity had been discovered and I was afraid Walter would make some trouble, so I suggested we both leave at once for Reno."

"What did she say?"

"She agreed."

"Did she pack a bag?"

"Just a little overnight bag, some creams and things. She changed her dress, and we left at once by the side entrance."

"Was there any conversation about what Mrs. Anderson might have seen?"

"There was. Mrs. Prescott felt certain Stella Anderson had been spying on us; that she'd seen what had taken place."

Stella Anderson jumped to her feet and exclaimed indignantly, "I wasn't spying! I never spy. I mind my own business and—"

The coroner's gavel banged into silence. "You'll have to be seated and keep quiet, Mrs. Anderson," he said, "or else leave the room."

Jimmy Driscoll seemed to pay no attention whatever to the interruption. With the air of a man who has an unpleasant duty to perform, but is determined to discharge it faithfully, he said, "Before our departure, we had some discussion about what we could do to prevent Mrs. Anderson from telling Walter Prescott what she had seen. Rosalind conceived the idea of having her sister come over, dress up in the same dress Mrs. Prescott had been wearing, and appear at the window where Mrs. Anderson could get a good look at her face. We telephoned Miss Swaine from the airport. I listened to Rosalind Prescott's conversation, and heard the instructions she gave Miss Swaine."

"Then what did you do?"

"Then we flew to Reno."

"Did you know Walter Prescott was dead at that time?"

"No—what's more," Driscoll said calmly, "I can prove that I didn't kill him, and that I didn't have anything to do with his death."

Cuff got to his feet belligerently and said, "I demand that my client be given an opportunity to prove his innocence."

"No one's stopping him," Scanlon said good-naturedly.

Overmeyer said, "I want the record to show, and Counsel to understand, the attitude of the district attorney's office is that of making an impartial, independent investigation. We're not trying to pin this crime on *anyone*. We want the facts, that's all."

"Go ahead," Rodney Cuff said to Driscoll.

Perry Mason stirred uneasily in his seat, started to say something, then lapsed into silence.

Driscoll said, "Walter Prescott was alive at eleven fifty-five. He telephoned his partner at that time. Five minutes later, just as the noon whistles were blowing, there was an automobile accident in front of Prescott's house. I ran out and helped remove the injured man from the coupe. I then returned to Prescott's house and gave Rosalind Prescott the gun with which, the evidence shows, the murder must have been committed. That gun was placed back of the drawer in the desk, and was subsequently found there by the police. Now, from that time until the time I left the house the witness, Stella Anderson, was watching that room. She didn't see anyone take the gun out from behind the drawer in the desk. At quarter past twelve Rosalind Prescott and I left the house by the side door—that's the one which opens on Fourteenth Street, and went to the airport, where we took the next plane out and went to Reno."

Emil Scanlon said very seductively, "That, of course, leaves a gap between eleven fifty-five and twelve o'clock. Not a great deal of time, to be certain, but one, nevertheless, within which a shot could easily have been fired."

Driscoll said, "During that time, I was engaged in telephoning."

"Could you prove that?" the deputy district attorney asked.

"Yes," Rodney Cuff said, answering for the witness. "If I may be allowed to call a witness I can prove my point."

Scanlon hesitated for a moment, glanced at the deputy district attorney, then at Rodney Cuff, then back to Oscar Overmeyer.

Overmeyer slowly, almost imperceptibly, nodded his head, and Emil Scanlon said, "Very well, we'll grant you permission to put on a witness. It's rather irregular to handle the thing in this way, but this is a peculiar case and we're anxious to get at what actually happened."

There was something of triumph in Rodney Cuff's manner as he got to his feet and said, "That's all, Mr. Driscoll. You may leave the stand for the moment and I'll call Jackson Weyman as my first witness."

A slender-built man in the early forties got to his feet and started to leave the room. "That's Weyman," Rodney Cuff said. "I want him as a witness."

An officer stopped Weyman at the door. Weyman turned and said, "I'm not going to be a witness. I didn't come here to be called to the witness stand."

His left eye was discolored and bloodshot. A piece of gauze, held in place by adhesive tape, covered the top of his forehead, and another smaller bit of tape was on his right cheek.

"I *demand* he be called as a witness," Cuff said.

"Come forward and be sworn, Mr. Weyman," the coroner ordered.

"I'm not going to do any such thing," Weyman said, his voice surly. "I don't want to be a witness, and you can't make me. I'm a hell of a looking specimen to get on the witness stand!"

The crowd roared with laughter, which Scanlon made no effort to check. When it had subsided, he said, "Come forward and be sworn, anyway, Mr. Weyman."

"I'm not going to tell anything," Weyman said doggedly.

The good-natured smile didn't leave the coroner's lips, but his eyes suddenly became hard. "I think," he said gently, "you're in error on that point, Mr. Weyman. Officer, bring him forward."

The officer took Weyman's arm and said, "Come on, buddy. This way."

Weyman, his temper flaring up, jumped back and lashed out a blow at the officer. The next instant he found himself grabbed with a strangle hold, spun neatly around, and then rushed down the corridor toward the witness chair, while the spectators set up a delighted tittering.

Scanlon said, "Hold him there just a minute, Mr. Officer. I want to say something to him. . . . Now, Mr. Weyman, this is an inquest. The coroner has the power to subpoena witnesses and make them testify. If you disobey me you're going to jail. I don't want to have any trouble, but if you know anything about this case, we're going to find it out. . . . Have you been drinking?"

Weyman said in a surly voice, "I've had a drink or two."

"Raise your right hand and be sworn," the coroner ordered sternly.

The officer released his hold, and Weyman, scowling savagely, raised his right hand and was sworn.

Scanlon indicated the witness chair, and Rodney Cuff stepped forward. "Mr. Weyman," he said, "you remember the automobile accident which took place in front of Walter Prescott's home?"

"Well, what if I do?"

"You live next door to Prescott?"

"Yes."

"And you saw that accident?"

"Yes, I saw it."

"Where were you at the time?"

"I was standing on Fourteenth Street."

"You'd been drinking, had picked a fight, and got the worst of the argument, is that right?"

"That's none of your damn business."

Scanlon banged with his gavel, frowned at the witness, but turned to Rodney Cuff and said, "This man is an unwilling witness. I'm forcing him to testify. I don't want him unnecessarily annoyed. What has his fighting got to do with it?"

"Simply this," Rodney Cuff said. "This witness has a habit of fighting when he's drunk. It's been a matter of argument between him and his wife. This time he'd been beaten into unconsciousness, had to go to a doctor to have his face dressed, and didn't want to go home and face the music. So he was standing rather uncertainly on Fourteenth Street near the corner of Alsace Avenue when the accident occurred. I want to show he was there at the time, and show why he was there."

"All right," Weyman said, in a surly voice, "that's right. I was there. So what?"

"You could see into Walter Prescott's house?"

"I could see through some of the windows on the Fourteenth Street side of the house."

"Could you see the little hallway where the telephone's located?"

"Yes, I could see that."

"Did you see Mr. Driscoll using the telephone?"

There was a moment of tense silence, when Weyman said reluctantly, "I seen a man standing there, telephoning. He had his back turned, though."

"Now you were standing there when the accident took place?"

"Yes."

"What was Driscoll doing when the accident took place?"

"The man I saw was still at the telephone."

"And how long had he been there?"

"I don't know, four or five minutes maybe."

"What did you do after the accident occurred?"

"I started to go over and see what had happened. Then I decided to keep out of it. I went back and sat down on the curb, watched them load the guy that was hurt into the van. This guy in the blue suit ran out and helped. Then he went back in the house, and I saw the van drive away."

"Then what?"

"Then, after a few minutes, I saw this man, Driscoll, come out of the house again. Just then a prowl car swung around the corner and the officers nailed this guy."

"How long did you stay there after that?"

"I didn't stay. I didn't want those officers asking me questions, so I beat it. I walked around for a while. I was kinda sleepy and wasn't feeling very good. After a while I made up my mind I had to face the music, so I turned around and went home."

"What time was that?"

"I don't know. It was long enough so I'd commenced to feel sick."

Rodney Cuff made a little gesture of surrendering the witness, and resumed his seat with a satisfied smile.

The coroner looked across at Overmeyer, and the deputy district attorney got to his feet, moved over toward the witness and said, "Could you be sure it was Mr. Driscoll you saw at the telephone?"

Weyman said in his thick, surly voice, "The telephone sets right up against the window. This guy was standing, leaning his shoulder against the side of the window. I could see his back and the back of his head. He had the same kind of black curly hair this Driscoll has. When he came out of the house I could see his face. The man who came out was Driscoll. I *know* that. I *think* he was the one who was telephoning."

"You'd been drinking at the time?"

"I'd had a few, yes."

"More than you've had now?"

There was a half smile on Weyman's face as he said, "A lot more."

"Are you positive about the time?"

Weyman shook his head and said, "No, I'm not. They told me the accident took place at noon. If that's true, then the rest of it's okay. If it ain't true, I don't know *what* time it was. All I know is I'd been standing around there for about ten minutes before the accident, and I saw this man telephoning."

Overmeyer frowned thoughtfully and said, "That's all. I may want to talk with you again about this, Mr. Weyman."

Mason said, "May I ask one question?"

Scanlon nodded.

"Whom have you told about what you saw?"

"I told my wife," Weyman said.

"Anyone else?"

Weyman shook his head.

"Did you tell her about this as soon as you got home?" Mason asked.

"No," Weyman said with a wry grin. "We talked about other things right after I got home."

Again a titter swept the room.

"That's all," Mason said.

Scanlon nodded to Weyman. "You're excused, Mr. Weyman," he said.

Rodney Cuff got to his feet and said, "I wish to point out that in view of the testimony of this witness, and the fact that we can show definitely the automobile accident took place almost exactly at the hour of noon, it was impossible for Jimmy Driscoll to have killed Walter Prescott.

"I think you can see what this means," Cuff went on, staring steadily at the deputy district attorney. "It means that sometime after Rosalind Prescott and my client had gone to Reno, and while Rita Swaine was in the house, Walter Prescott arrived. I won't presume to conjecture what happened, but Rita Swaine killed him. From what my client tells me of Rita Swaine, I presume that the provocation was great. Perhaps it was self-defense, or—"

"If Counsel is going to make an argument," Perry Mason said casually, "*I* want to make one."

"He isn't going to make one," Scanlon ruled. "Sit down, Mr. Cuff."

"I merely wanted to point out that—"

"You've already pointed out plenty. Sit down."

Oscar Overmeyer frowned thoughtfully, looked up at the coroner and said, "I had intended to prove by the canary itself that it probably wasn't Rita Swaine whom Mrs. Anderson had seen in the solarium. The admission of the witness Driscoll makes this unnecessary."

Mason said, "In view of what has been said by Counsel, I'd like permission to recall the autopsy surgeon for a few questions."

"No objection," Overmeyer said. "My office wants to get to the bottom of this thing as well as the coroner."

"The coroner's *going* to get to the bottom of it," Scanlon said cheerfully. "Dr. Hubert, take the stand again."

When the doctor had seated himself, Mason said, "In view of the statements which have been made, Doctor, I think you can well appreciate the importance of being absolutely accurate in your testimony as to the time of death. You have already answered this question in effect, but in view of the importance which now attaches to this phase of the case, I want to ask you again: Is it possible that Walter Prescott could have met his death earlier than within the time limits you have previously mentioned?"

Dr. Hubert crossed his legs, interlaced his fingers upon a paunchy stomach, cleared his throat and said, "I don't want to be misunderstood. Medical testimony as to the time of death is never absolutely mathematical. There are certain variable factors the exact nature and extent of which cannot be intelligently correlated. Therefore, an autopsy surgeon fixes a probable time of death. Then, taking into consideration all of the variable factors, he creates a margin of probability on either side of the time chosen. If he is conscientious, he extends this margin of probability so that it covers every possible combination of variable factors. Then he announces the time of death in terms of a time bracket."

"You did this?" Mason asked.

"Yes."

"And when you said that the time of death occurred between noon and two-thirty in the afternoon, do I understand that you estimated, purely as a matter of blind reckoning, that the decedent met his death at approximately one-fifteen; that it was possible, however, certain variable factors, as you have termed them, might have caused an error in your deduction; that you, therefore, made a maximum allowance of one hour and fifteen minutes in either direction as the greatest possible margin of error in your time fixing?"

"That's approximately correct," Dr. Hubert said. "Personally, I would say the man was killed between one and one-thirty. Eight or nine times out of ten, I'd be right. But there's the possibility of a combination of various circumstances which would impair the conclusion in perhaps one out of ten times. So I've taken that into consideration, and extended the margins far enough both ways so as to include even that one time in ten."

"And can you say that twelve o'clock is the earliest possible time at which the decedent could have met his death?"

"Yes."

"According to your own testimony, Doctor, the man could have died at one minute past twelve, noon."

"That's right."

"He *could* have died at noon?"

"Yes, sir."

"But he couldn't have met his death at eleven fifty-nine?"

"Oh, I say," Dr. Hubert said, "that's rather an unfair way of putting it."

"*I* don't think so," Mason said.

"Well, yes, of course," Dr. Hubert said, somewhat testily, "if you're going to split hairs that fine, if the man could have died at twelve o'clock, he could also have died at eleven fifty-nine. I don't think he did, but he could have."

"How about eleven forty-five?"

"A witness heard him speaking on the telephone at eleven fifty-five," Dr. Hubert pointed out acidly.

"Exactly," Mason said. "Now you have my point exactly, Doctor. When you fix the earliest time at which the man could have met his death as around twelve o'clock, you're taking into consideration that the man, according to the testimony of one witness, had been alive at eleven fifty-five, isn't that right?"

"No."

"Yet, when I ask you if it isn't a medical possibliity that the man could have been killed at eleven forty-five, you answer me by pointing out that according to the testimony of a witness, he was alive at eleven fifty-five. Now then, Doctor, are you testifying as to your medical knowledge, or as to an opinion formed by taking into unconscious consideration the testimony of witnesses?"

"I'm testifying as to a medical opinion formed from a post-mortem examination of the decedent."

"Let's get at it in another way, Doctor. You have mentioned one case in ten in which a combination of variable factors might necessitate moving the time bracket over a wider range. Now, isn't it possible that there is, perhaps, one case in a thousand, or one case in ten thousand, which would necessitate moving the brackets over a still wider range than would be covered by that one case in ten which you mentioned?"

"Oh, all right," Dr. Hubert said, "if you want to put it that way, let's say that he died between eleven-thirty in the morning and three o'clock in the afternoon, and I'll stake my professional reputation he died *within* those times, and couldn't have died as early as eleven twenty-nine. Does that satisfy you?"

"It isn't a question of satisfying me," Mason pointed out. "It's a question of getting at the facts."

"Well, you've got at them now," Dr. Hubert said.

Scanlon nodded and said, "I think we, all of us, understand the facts. You're excused, Doctor."

There was a moment of silence. Then the coroner said, "In view of the circumstances, I want to recall Mr. Driscoll for one more question."

"Take the stand, Driscoll," Rodney Cuff said.

Scanlon stared at the young man with steady, purposeful eyes. "Is it possible that someone else could have been in the Prescott house while you were there, Mr. Driscoll?"

Driscoll shook his head. "I think not, your Honor."

Scanlon's voice became utterly without emphasis or expression. "Did you," he asked, "go into all the rooms in that house?"

"Well," Driscoll said, hesitated, then went on quickly, "of course we didn't go into the upstairs bedrooms, no, sir."

"You're positive of that?"

"Quite!" Driscoll snapped.

"And you didn't go into the basement?"

"No, if there is a basement I didn't go into it."

"It is, then, quite possible some other person was in the house at the time, and without your knowledge?"

"Yes," Driscoll said, but added, "Such a person, however, couldn't have taken that revolver from my possession, fired three shots into Walter Prescott and returned the revolver to my pocket without my knowing it. In the event Prescott was killed with my gun, he was killed at some time after I had left the house."

"I understand your point perfectly," Scanlon said. "That's all, Mr. Driscoll. You're excused."

Less than ten minutes later, the coroner's jury brought in its verdict, finding that Walter Prescott had been shot to death by person or persons unknown. Rodney Cuff, sauntering over toward Perry Mason, said, "How do you like the verdict, Counselor?"

"*Should* I like it?" Mason asked.

Cuff nodded and said, "*I* think so. *I* like it fine."

"One thing," Mason commented, "is that when you

see Mr. Dimmick in the morning you can tell him that, in my opinion, he has no cause for worry at the quality of representation you will give young Driscoll. Having him go on the stand and admit the plot to substitute Rita Swaine for Rosalind Prescott is rather a stroke of genius."

"Yes," Cuff said, his expression bland. "You see, I'd heard that the district attorney's investigators had taken charge of the canary, and I deduced that could mean only one thing. Thanks to your clever deductive reasoning, Driscoll knew the jig was up, and told me the circumstances frankly, where he might otherwise have tried to conceal them."

"How did you know about Weyman as a witness?" Mason asked.

Cuff laughed. "He told his wife, and his wife told Stella Anderson, and she keeps a secret like a sieve holds water. I felt I could call him unexpectedly and make a better impression than if I'd talked with him and introduced him as a willing witness."

Mason nodded, lit a cigarette and said, "How do you suppose Rosalind's going to feel when she learns that Driscoll tried to divert suspicion from himself by involving Rita Swaine?"

"You surely don't think he did that?" Cuff asked.

"Yes, he did exactly that."

Cuff thought for a moment, then said, "One thing you may be overlooking, Mr. Mason: Before this inquest started, the district attorney was preparing extradition proceedings against *both* Rita Swaine and Rosalind Prescott. As matters now stand, he will proceed to extradite Rita Swaine. He can't extradite Rosalind Prescott—not in the face of this evidence."

"And you think that's a good thing?" Mason asked.

"I think so, yes."

"For whom?"

"For Rosalind Prescott, primarily."

"How about Miss Swaine?" Mason inquired.

"Miss Swaine," Cuff told him, "will have to take care of herself—with your very able assistance."

Mason nodded, said, "I gathered as much. You know, Cuff, there's just one disadvantage about having your client stage this cards-on-the-table act."

"What's that?" Cuff asked.

"God help him if he's lying," Mason said grimly.

CHAPTER ELEVEN

RITA SWAINE sat across from Perry Mason in the visitor's room in the county jail. A long row of heavy wire mesh divided the table into two parts. Rita sat on one side, and Mason on the other.

"Can I talk here?" she asked.

"Keep your voice low," Mason said, "and, above all, don't get excited. People are watching us. Make your manner casual. No matter what you tell me, shake your head once or twice emphatically, as though denying your guilt. Now, go ahead and tell me the truth."

"Rosalind killed him," she said.

"How do you know? Did she say so?"

"No, not in so many words. Oh, it's awful. She's my own sister, and now she's turned against me. She and Jimmy Driscoll did it and she's willing to have Jimmy make me the goat because she loves him so much she can't bear the thought of anything happening to him, and he's pushing it all over on me just to save his own skin."

"How do you know they killed him?" Mason asked.

"Because," she said, "they did. Walter came in and caught Jimmy there, and Jimmy shot him."

"Go ahead," Mason told her, his voice a low, rumbling monotone. "Tell me what you know. But shake your head first—that's it."

"Rossy called me over the telephone, said something

awful had happened and asked me to go over to her house right away. I told her I couldn't go right at that moment. So then she told me to go down to the pay station in the drug store and call a certain number. She did that because she didn't want to take chances on having the clerk at the switchboard hear what we were talking about."

"All right," Mason said, "you went to the drug store and called her. Where was she?"

"She was at the airport then. She told me that Jimmy had been there in the house with her; that he'd taken her in his arms and made passionate love to her; that there'd been an auto accident out front and the police had made Jimmy give them his name and address and that he'd be called on as a witness. She said that Jimmy had given her a gun right after the accident and before he'd run into the police; that she'd dropped the gun down in back of a drawer in the desk in the solarium. Then she said Jimmy had tried to leave, had run into the police, and had decided the only thing to do was to run away with her; that Mrs. Snoops had seen everything and she'd undoubtedly tell Walter."

"So what did you do?" Mason said.

"She gave me all the details, told me that she'd left the dress she'd been wearing in the bedroom and that the canary was fluttering around the solarium.

"Well, of course, I told her I'd go over and put on an act for the benefit of Mrs. Snoops. I didn't want to do it particularly, because I was afraid I might run into Walter. But she told me she knew absolutely Walter wouldn't be there."

"Did she tell you how she knew?" Mason asked.

"No."

"So you went over there?" Mason inquired. "And then what?"

"When I went to the upstairs bedroom to change into the dress Rossy had been wearing, I found the door to Walter's bedroom slightly ajar. I didn't think anything of it at the moment, left my dress there, put on Rossy's, went down to the solarium, caught the canary, and did my stuff where Mrs. Snoops could get an eyeful. Then I went back upstairs to change my dress again. I went into the bathroom to wash my hands, and got a shock. There were bloodstains on the wash bowl—not stains of pure blood, but places where drops of bloody water had dried on the porcelain, leaving little pinkish stains, and in some places the drops hadn't dried.

"So I pushed open the door, looked in Walter's bedroom, and there was Walter, lying on his bed, on his back, his arms outstretched, his vest unbuttoned, and blood flowing from bullet wounds. I stood there on the threshold and screamed. Then, after a moment, I cried out, 'Walter, what's the matter?' and ran across to the bed, knelt by his side and put my hands on his shoulders.

"I knew right away that he was dead."

She paused, breathing heavily through dilated nostrils. Her lips quivered.

"Go ahead," Mason told her. "Give me the rest of it."

"Honestly, Mr. Mason, I don't know what made me do the thing I did next. At first I was so shocked and horrified I could hardly breathe. And then, all of a sudden, I seemed to adjust myself in relation to what it would mean to me and to Rossy—"

"Never mind the psychology," Mason said. "What did you *do*?"

"I thought about that letter Jimmy had written. I knew that Walter had planned to file suit against Jimmy and I knew what it would mean to Rossy if they should search the body, find that letter and—"

"What did you *do*?" Mason interrupted.

"I opened his inner pocket, took out his wallet and looked for the letter."

"Did you find it?"

"Yes."

"What did you do with it?"

"Folded it and put it in the top of my stocking."

"You were wearing Rosalind's dress at the time?"

"No, I'd taken off the dress."

"Were you wearing a slip?"

"Not then. I put one on later."

"How long was it before you took that letter out of your stocking?"

"After I'd got downstairs."

"What did you do with it?"

"Burnt it in the fireplace."

"How did you burn it?"

"Why," she said, "I touched a match to it. How does anyone ever burn things?"

"That isn't what I mean. What did you do with the ashes?"

"Why, left them in the fireplace, of course."

"Did you take a poker or a stick or anything and break them up?"

"No, I set fire to the letter, saw it was burning, and then tossed it into the fireplace. It flamed up all at once and singed my hair a little."

"How were you dressed at the time?"

"I had on my gray suit."

"The same one you wore to my office?"

"Yes."

"What else did you do?"

"I took the canary and came to you. That's why I came to you, Mr. Mason. Rossy hadn't wanted me to get her a lawyer. She just wanted me to put on the act for Mrs. Snoops, but I felt she needed someone to protect her interests."

"In other words, you knew there was going to be a murder case when you came to me?"

"Yes."

"Then you flew to Reno?"

"That's right."

"And then what?"

"I was waiting to have a talk with Rossy after Jimmy had gone to bed and I could talk with her alone. I told her I'd arranged for you to be her lawyer, and I'd told her about Mrs. Snoops. I didn't tell her about Walter, or ask her about the murder. I knew Rossy wouldn't have done it. Jimmy did it, and Rossy's backing him up. I wanted to ask her about it when Jimmy wasn't there to make her lie."

"Where's your pearl-gray outfit now?" Mason asked.

"The police took it. They made me change to other clothes."

"How about the shoes you were wearing?"

"They have them."

"Did you look them over for bloodstains?"

"No, I didn't—good heavens, Mr. Mason, you don't think I—"

"I think," he told her, "that you very probably had bloodstains on your shoes. You may have had some on your undergarments. I think that you left your finger-prints on the wallet in Walter Prescott's pocket, and if you didn't break up the ashes in the fireplace, I think they'll find enough of the letter to photograph."

"Do you mean to say they can photograph a letter after it's been burnt?"

"Yes," Mason said. "With the use of modern photography and ultra-violet and infra-red light, they can photograph writing on charred paper with the greatest accuracy. I *thought* Overmeyer was acting a little too dumb at the inquest. He had so much against you that he didn't want to tip his hand in advance. He's perfectly willing to let the coroner's verdict be indefinite. He wants you to think he hasn't very much evidence, and then get you lying. Did you make any statements?"

"No," she said, "I remembered what you'd told me and didn't say anything."

"Did you make any denials?"

"Oh, yes," she said. "They accused me of killing Walter, and I denied I'd done that."

Mason frowned and said irritably, "I told you not to say anything."

"Well, I thought I should deny *that*."

"Did you," he asked, "go one step farther and deny knowing that he was dead?"

"No. I simply sat tight after that one denial."

"Did they ask you when you'd seen him last?"

"Yes," she said, "they did, and I told them I hadn't seen him for a week. That was right, because I hadn't. It really doesn't count seeing a man after he's dead, and—"

"And," Mason interrupted, "when the finger-print expert hangs an enlarged photograph of your finger-prints found on Walter's wallet up in front of the jury, you'll have plenty of time to think over how much better it would have been to have followed your lawyer's advice."

Her eyes were wide and frightened, as the full meaning of his remark penetrated her consciousness. Then her chin came up and she said, "All right, *you* don't need to rub it in. It's no skin off your nose."

"Did you kill him?"

"No."

"Do you know who did?"

"I— No . . . unless Rossy did."

"If you're lying to me," Mason said brutally, "they're going to put a coarse hemp rope around that pretty neck of yours and drop you through a trap—and they may do it anyway."

"I'm not lying. And, after all, Mr. Perry Mason, it's *my* neck."

Mason's eyes showed approval. "Well," he said, "you can take it, anyhow. That's a lot better than having a woman on my hands who'll get hysterical and go to pieces on the witness stand. Now, get this, and get it straight. The district attorney will start springing stuff on you. First, he'll pretend that he hasn't any case against you, is holding you more or less on suspicion, and that if you'd only deny the charges against you he'd probably turn you loose, but he can't do it in the face of public opinion while you're refusing to make any comments. Then, after he lures you into making a few more statements, denying this, that and the other, he'll start springing evidence on you and ask you to explain that. He'll do it all in a fatherly sort of manner and pretend that your release is just around the corner. Then, as you keep getting in deeper and deeper, he'll start tightening the screws a little at a time, until you finally find yourself in a blind panic. Then, when you quit talking to him, he'll turn the newspaper people loose on you and they'll use all the wiles of the profession in order to get you talking. They'll tell you what a powerful factor public opinion is. They'll tell you how much good it'll do your side of the case if their sob sisters dress up a swell story of how you tried to protect your sister and inadvertently got involved in a murder charge. They'll tell you how nice it'll be for you if your name is kept before the public, how they'll give a prominent position to your interview, a sympathetic treatment to your story; how they'll pay you to publish your memoirs or your diary. And they'll use a hundred other different arguments to get you to talk. Do you understand?"

She nodded.

"Now," Mason said, "you're going to keep quiet all the way along the line. With the evidence the district attorney has against you, he'll never release you. The only way you'll ever get out of jail is by having a jury say 'Not guilty,' or having three juries in a row fail to agree on a verdict. Do you understand that?"

Again she nodded.

"All right," Mason said. "Whenever anyone asks you to say anything, whether it's district attorney or news-paper man, or some very sympathetic fellow-prisoner who just 'happens' to be put in the same cell with you, you'll say that you want to talk; that I've ordered you not to talk; that as long as I'm your attorney, you're going to obey orders; that you think it's all foolishness; that you want to tell your story in a simple, straightforward manner, but that for some reason I'm ordering you to keep quiet. In other words, you pass the buck, and pass it big. Do you get that?"

"I get it," she said.

"Do you have nerve enough to do it?"

"I think so."

"It's going to take a lot of will power."

She said, "I know all about that, too. After all, Mr.

Mason, I'm twenty-seven years old. A girl develops will power in twenty-seven years."

"Bosh!" he told her. "You've been out with some young sprout who's tried to do a little necking in an amateurish way and you think you've built up a mental discipline and an ability to take care of yourself. You're going up against *men* now, men who have handled so many hundred similar cases that it's a matter of routine with them. They know all the tricks that work, and those that don't work. You're a babe in the woods, going up against it for the first time. Keep your mouth shut, except for that one statement about wanting to talk but not being allowed to. Do you understand?"

"Yes," she said, her eyes indignant, "I understand. And don't think young men are as amateurish as your little speech would imply."

Mason got to his feet, started to turn away from the screen, then swung back to sit down once more. "How far can I go with this thing?" he asked.

"What do you mean?"

"You know what I mean."

"Don't involve Rossy," she said.

"Suppose I have to drag Rossy in to get you out?" he inquired, watching her narrowly.

"Then don't get me out."

"Do you know what you're saying?"

"Of course I do."

"You're in bad," Mason said, "Plenty bad. Anything may happen. With your looks, your brain and your figure, a jury isn't apt to hang you. You may get life imprisonment. You may get a first-degree murder verdict without any recommendation, which will automatically mean the death penalty. It's all right now for you to stick your chin up and tell me to keep Rossy out of it, but what'll happen when the zero hour comes? Will you reproach me for letting you tie my hands?"

She got to her feet then, stood facing him across the screened table. "Mr. Mason," she said, "when I do anything, I do it wholeheartedly, and I'm not inclined to regret it afterwards, no matter what the circumstances are. That's my code of life. Lots of people live namby-pamby littles lives, in which they try to blame their mistakes on someone else. I don't. You've asked me if I can take it. Now I'm asking you if you can take it."

Mason grinned, said, "Okay, Rita, I'm going places."

Rita Swaine watched the jail matron moving toward her, smiled gamely and said, "I'm not."

CHAPTER TWELVE

ROSALIND PRESCOTT sat in Perry Mason's office, clenched her little gloved hands until the soft leather grew tight across the knuckles, and said fiercely, "No, I didn't kill him! I tell you I didn't. I didn't! I didn't! I didn't!"

"Who did?"

"I don't know. I wish I did."

"Suppose you did know, then what?"

Her eyes were hard, as they met Mason's. "I'd tell the police."

"Suppose Rita did it?"

"What makes you think Rita did it?"

"That isn't what I said. I asked you what your attitude would be *if* Rita had killed him."

"If Rita killed him," she said, "she isn't entitled to any consideration from Jimmy or from me. She put us both in an awful spot."

"Suppose Jimmy killed him?"

"If Jimmy killed him he isn't entitled to any more consideration—well, hardly any more—well—"

Mason nodded and said, "So it's different if Jimmy killed him, is it?"

"Well," she said hotly, "if Jimmy killed him, he had some reason. He had plenty of reason."

"Did Rita have any reason?"

"I don't know. If she did it, it was probably in self-defense."

"Isn't that a good reason?" Mason asked.

"Yes. The reason's all right, but it's the way she handled it, sneaking out and leaving the body in such a way that Jimmy would be blamed for it."

"And if Driscoll did it, then what?"

"Jimmy did it to protect me—but he didn't do it—that is, I don't think he did it."

"Did Mrs. Anderson have any grudge against Walter Prescott?"

Her eyes opened wide with surprise. "Why, Mr. Mason! What makes you ask that?"

"I'm just trying to cover every angle of the case," he said. "Also, I'm trying to cover every possible defense which we might raise. Did she have anything against him?"

"I don't think so. Of course, Walter had objected to her snooping around. He'd told her a couple of times to mind her own business and quit peering into our windows, and she told him he could keep the shades drawn if he didn't want her to see him. She said she wasn't going around *her* house and pull down all the shades at night."

"Was it much of a battle?" Mason asked.

"Not particularly. She's snippy, and Walter was very sarcastic."

"And that's all she had against him?"

"All that I know of, yes."

"Now, your husband had threatened to kill you?"

"Yes."

"Many times?"

"Twice. The first time was a couple of months ago over something which needn't make any difference here. The last time was the morning when I ran away."

"Why did you go to Reno?"

"I had an idea of establishing a residence there and getting a divorce. I thought if I were out of the state Walter wouldn't do anything right away, and after he'd had a chance to cool off, I might be able to fix things up with him so there wouldn't be a scandal."

"You went with Driscoll?"

"Yes."

"You knew he was jealous of Driscoll?"

"He wasn't jealous of anyone. He was just a cold-blooded, selfish, calculating—"

"Wait a minute," Mason interrupted. "That isn't going to be the attitude you'll take on the witness stand. Cut out that vicious hatred when you speak of Walter Prescott. Remember, he's dead."

"I don't care whether he's dead or alive. He was—"

"He was your husband," Mason interrupted. "You had differences of opinion with him. It had occurred to you for some time that you no longer cared for him; that you'd been tricked into marrying him, but you felt sorry for him. Understand that. Your attitude was one of sympathy and compassion. You realized that, while at times he was intensely disagreeable, it was because of his peculiar nervous temperament."

"It was because he had a cold heart and a selfish, calculating disposition," she said.

"And," Mason went on, heedless of her comment, "it was a great shock to you when you learned he was dead, just as it would be a shock to hear that anyone who had been close to you had passed away. You weren't overcome by grief because you realized you didn't love him, but you were shocked, and deeply grieved. Hundreds of thousands of marriages go on the rocks every year, but that doesn't mean that either or both parties to the divorce action are not ordinary likeable human beings. It simply means that emotions don't remain static; that love, like any other fire, will burn itself out unless fresh fuel is added, and many people don't understand the art of adding fresh fuel to romance, once the romance has culminated in marriage."

She said, "You want me to say that?"

"Words to that effect," he told her.

"On the witness stand?"

"You probably won't be asked on the witness stand. But long before you get into court you'll be interviewed by newspaper men and—"

"I've already been interviewed," she said. "Plenty!"

"What did you tell them?"

"Nothing. You told me to say nothing, and that's exactly what I did."

"All right," he told her. "We're going to change that now. You're going to talk, and you're going to talk freely. You just can't believe that Rita could possibly have done any such thing, although you didn't have an opportunity to discuss with Rita exactly what had happened after you left the house. Remember, you're to tell all the newspaper people that you and Rita didn't discuss what occurred while she was there in the house."

Rosalind Prescott nodded.

"You'll admit frankly that you love Jimmy Driscoll. In fact, you'll spread that on rather thick. Remember, all the world loves a lover. But be sure that it's romance and not the marital transgression of a restless woman. You had loved Jimmy; then you had quarreled. You had resolutely put Jimmy out of your life and endeavored by every means to make your marriage a success. Gradually the veneer had worn off. You came to see that you and Walter weren't suited for each other. No matter how much he might have meant to others, he couldn't fill your life. And he didn't try. Your married life became sort of a cat-and-dog existence. You were desperately unhappy. During all of this time the thought of Jimmy Driscoll hadn't come to your mind except as a friend. Then he wrote to you, not as a lover, but as a friend, a friend who had handled all your financial matters. He told you that it would be better to make the break and get it over with and not try to prolong a hopeless situation. Then, when Jimmy came to the house and you looked in his eyes, you suddenly realized that you loved him and always had loved him. But that was after you had realized that you could never continue living with Walter Prescott: after you had both agreed to split up and obtain a divorce. Do you understand that?"

"What do I say about the twelve thousand dollars?"

"Absolutely nothing," Mason said, "other than that you gave Walter some money to invest. His untimely death prevented you two from having a financial accounting."

"That's what I say, but what about the twelve thousand dollars?" she demanded.

"It doesn't make any difference now," Mason told her. "You inherit whatever property there is. Now that the authorities have decided not to prosecute you on a murder charge, I'm filing application for letters of administration. Are there any relatives?"

"No. Otherwise he'd have willed everything to them. In any event, he—"

"Forget it," Mason interrupted. "Remember that Walter was nervous. Walter was working too hard. Walter was a man who cared nothing for society or companionship, but only because he was too self-sufficient. The fact that you didn't get along with him doesn't mean there was anything wrong with his character."

She said venomously, "I hate to lie. He embezzled my money. He was a—"

"Never mind what he was," Mason said. "He's dead. You remember what I told you about him. Keep that attitude whenever you speak of him. He left no relatives, and you as his wife inherit all of his property, whether it's separate or community. You'll get your twelve thousand back that way."

The private telephone on his desk jangled into noise. Only three people had the number of that telephone. It was used only in the event of major emergencies.

Mason scooped the receiver to his ear and heard Drake's voice saying, "Sorry to call you on this line, Perry, but this is important as hell. I think we've found Jason Braun, or Carl Packard, whichever you want to call him."

"Where?" Mason asked.

"Out in the country. I'm having a man bring up a car."

"Where are you now?"

"Just leaving the office. I'll meet you at the elevator."

Mason said, "Okay," banged up the receiver, pushed back his chair, called over his shoulder to Rosalind Prescott, "Be back in an hour. In the meantime, remember what I told you. Change your attitude to the newspaper boys. Talk plenty, but don't tell them anything."

Della Street scooped her notebook and pencils into a handbag, said, "Do you want me, Chief?"

He shook his head and said, "Go over Mrs. Prescott's story with her a little. Pretend you're a newspaper woman. Ask her questions and get her answers. I'll either be back in an hour or telephone you."

He grabbed his hat, jerked open the corridor door, and strode down the flagged floor. Drake was waiting for him at the elevator.

"What is it?" Mason asked.

"It's reported as an automobile accident," Drake said. "It went in through the traffic department. I don't think the police have taken a tumble yet."

"What sort of an accident?"

"Car rolled over a grade out in the mountains between Santa Monica and Triumfo. It's been down at the bottom of the canyon for a couple of days."

"The man that drove it?" Mason asked.

"Under the car. Smashed flatter than a pancake."

The elevator slid to a stop. Drake started to say something as they stepped into the cage, but Mason said, "Save it, Paul," and glanced significantly at the elevator operator.

Not until they were speeding out Wilshire Boulevard in a car driven by one of Drake's men did the detective give any details to the attorney. "This report came in to the Highway Department. I won't bother you with details, Perry, but one of the possibilities I'd figured on was that this chap, Packard, had disappeared because something had happened to him. So I'd assigned men to look into every murder and accident case, as well as every automobile accident. As soon as a report came in, my man chased out to the scene of the accident. He found out this fellow's hat had the imprint of a haberdashery store in

Altaville in the band, and that the initials 'C.P.' had
been stamped in the band. There seemed to have been no
papers of identification in the pockets. From all I can
understand, the corpse is pretty much of a mess. However,
we can make an identification from finger-prints. The
Board of Fire Underwriters had all of their men fingerprinted, and I managed to secure a copy of Jason Braun's
prints."

Mason said, "Of course, Paul, if the man's dead, it isn't
going to do us any good to discover him in advance of the
police, unless there are some circumstances in connection
with his death which would give us a clue. After all, the
thing I want is to find out what this man saw in the
window of the Prescott house which distracted his attention and sent him crashing into that van."

"Well," Drake said, "I figured we'd get on the job, find
out all we could, and perhaps take some photographs. I
brought a camera along."

"Where's the place?"

"Up in the mountains. We go out to Santa Monica,
start up the coast boulevard toward Oxnard, and then
turn off on one of the side roads. My man will be waiting at the intersection to flag us down."

Mason lit a cigarette, smoked thoughtfully for a moment while the driver, swinging to the outside lane of
traffic, sent the speedometer needle quivering upward.

"Incidentally," Drake said, "I've found out why the
police took such prompt steps when the report came in
about Stella Anderson having seen the man hiding the
gun."

"Shoot."

"Prescott had telephoned the police that he had reason
to believe someone was going to try to kill him, but
couldn't, or wouldn't, say who that someone was. The
police asked him a few questions, and, among other things,
wanted to know if he wanted a permit to carry a gun.
He said he didn't, but said there'd been a prowler around
the house for a couple of nights, and if he should telephone the police, he wanted quick action. He said he kept

a double-barreled shot-gun in the house and said he wasn't going to take any chances; that if anyone tried to break in he was going to cut loose with his shot-gun."

"That sounds phony," Mason said. "It doesn't ring true."

"I know it doesn't," Drake told him, "but that's why the police paid attention to the report that came in about Driscoll giving a gun to the girl to hide."

Mason said thoughtfully, "I wonder if he thought Jimmy Driscoll was going to be hanging around the house, and he could lay a foundation with a complaint to the police, and then spray Driscoll full of lead."

"If we're guessing," Drake said, "it sounds like a good guess."

Mason smoked in silence for half a dozen blocks, then said meditatively, "Well, we're guessing. . . . Paul, there's something phony about Walter Prescott. I can't put my finger on just what it is, but somehow he doesn't ring true. This business of taking money from his wife to invest in the business, and salting it away—the large deposits which he apparently made in the bank, notwithstanding the relatively small amounts he took out of his business— By the way, Trader mentioned he was delivering some stuff to Prescott's garage. I wonder just what that stuff was. Suppose you check into that angle?"

"But he had the accident and went right on to the hospital," Drake said "—No, you're right, at that, Perry, he *did* make the delivery later. I remember now. He said he left the hospital to come back to the garage."

"Prescott, you'll remember," Mason told him, "had given Trader his keys."

"That's right."

"So Trader had a key to the garage door."

"I wonder what happened to those keys," Drake remarked. "Trader's never accounted for them, as far as I can find."

"Might be a good plan to give him a little more shakedown."

"Getting information out of Trader," Drake said, "is like getting blood out of a turnip."

Mason nodded. "He left the hospital before Packard was discharged. Packard was there about thirty-five minutes. He arrived there about ten minutes past twelve. That means Trader must have delivered the merchandise some time around quarter to one or one o'clock."

"That would have been before Rita Swaine arrived?" Drake asked.

Mason nodded and said, "The more I think of it, Paul, the more I think I'm interested in knowing just what that merchandise consisted of. Trader didn't want to give us any information when we talked with him, but now there's been a murder, the situation will be different."

Drake pulled out his notebook, braced himself against the swaying of the automobile, tried in vain to write legibly. He looked at the scrawled letters, grinned and said, "When I see something I can't read, I'll know that means 'look up merchandise in the garage.'"

Mason settled back against the cushions. "What did you find out about Prescott?" he asked the detective.

"Plenty," Drake said. "I can tell you all about him from the time he left kindergarten until he was found dead. I could even give you some of his grades in school."

"How was he, bright?"

"Not particularly during grammar school. He took a spurt in high school, and made a pretty good record in college. He was a chemical engineer. Then he drifted into insurance adjusting."

"How about his personality?"

"Rotten," Drake said. "He made very few friends, either in college or outside. George Wray was the business producer in the firm. Prescott was a walking encyclopedia of miscellaneous information. He had a great mind for detail. He was valuable when it came to taking care of the business Wray brought in."

"What about Driscoll?" the lawyer asked.

"Just a nice rich play-boy. His mother died when he was fifteen. She left an estate of around a couple of million, mostly in the form of cash. It's all tied up in a complicated trust, administered by the bank. Driscoll can't touch the principal until he's thirty-five. The income goes to him in accordance with the terms of the trust, one of which is that he can't have more than three hundred dollars a month unless he earns more than three hundred dollars a month in some gainful and legitimate occupation. Then he can get more—but that's at the discretion of the trustees again."

"Sounds as though the boy had some defect of character," Mason said. "From the time he's fifteen until the time he's thirty-five is a long time."

"I know," Drake said, "but apparently it was his mother's idea that he was going to have to work and learn something of the value of money before he started playing around with the estate. You see, she put it right up to him. He couldn't be much of a man-about-town on three hundred a month. But if he earned three hundred dollars a month, then the trustees could turn over as much or as little of the income as they thought advisable. I think it was drink she was afraid of, I don't know. Anyway, she sure put a fence around the kid."

"How did she happen to pick on Dimmick, Gray & Peabody?"

"They'd been her lawyers for years. They drew up the trust. And, incidentally, picked off a sweet thing for the bank. That's the way they do. The bank turns them an estate every once in a while, and they turn the bank a nice piece of trust business."

"Mrs. Driscoll evidently had a lot of confidence in Abner Dimmick."

"She did. He was the one who had the contact with her. It was partnership business, but Dimmick was the one she always asked for. Incidentally," Drake said, "that young chap, Cuff, did a pretty good job of representing Driscoll, didn't he?"

Mason frowned thoughtfully and said, "I wish I knew. He was either practicing law by ear and happened to make a good guess, or else he's one of those natural courtroom lawyers we hear about but seldom see. He rather forcibly impressed on me that the authorities couldn't extradite Rosalind Prescott and that it might be a good move on my part to keep her outside of the state."

"But," Drake said, "that would swing public opinion very strongly against her."

"I'm not certain but what that's what he was trying to do," Mason said. "You see, his manner contrasts very much with my own. I sit in court with an armful of legal monkey-wrenches and toss them into the machinery whenever I see a couple of wheels getting ready to move around. Cuff is one of those chaps who apparently wants to co-operate all the time. He was so nice down there at the inquest that butter wouldn't melt in his mouth. Yet he managed to squeeze out from under and leave Rita Swaine holding the sack."

They rode for a while in silence. Then Drake asked, "What was your hunch on the redhead in Prescott's office, Perry?"

"I just thought she'd bear investigation, that's all. Why, did you find out anything?"

"She's leading a double life," Drake said, grinning. "I know that much."

"What's the double life?"

"Daytimes she's Rosa Hendrix. She works at the office under that name, goes home to a thirty-four-dollar-a-month apartment at 1025 Alvord Avenue. She stays there for half an hour or so, then calls a taxi and goes to apartment 5-C in the Bellefontaine, one of the swankiest apartment houses in the city."

"And what does she do there?"

"Spends the night, apparently, then goes to the Alvord Avenue address and then to work."

"But what's the idea?" Mason asked.

"Darned if I know," Drake told him. "I haven't been on the job long enough to know."

"Some man paying for the apartment in the Belle-fontaine?"

"Apparently not. She keeps it under the name of Diana Morgan, has a few boy-friends who drop in to see her, but no more than could be expected with a respectable young woman. Everything's handled very discreetly and aboveboard. But occasionally she announces she's going to take a trip down to Mexico, up to San Francisco, or over to Reno. She sends a transfer man up, has her trunks taken down to the depot, and doesn't show up for a week or so. Then she comes back with her procession of trunks, and settles down to routine life."

"What does she do while she's gone?" Mason asked.

"Apparently just keeps on working at Prescott & Wray's office for a salary of a hundred and twenty-five dollars a month. Incidentally, the apartment in the Bellefontaine costs her three hundred and ninety-five."

Mason puckered his forehead into thought.

"Does that add up and make sense?" Drake asked. "You know, she could be a phony, but still not have anything to do with *this* case."

Mason nodded thoughtfully. "She *could,*" he said, "but all the way through this case there's been something screwy, something which just didn't make sense. So, under the circumstances, we're going to dig into everything that looks the least big irregular. I hate to pry into Rosa Hendrix's private love-life, Paul, but I want a complete report on everything she does."

"I'm watching her like a hawk," Drake told him. "It happens that the manager of the Bellefontaine is a client of mine. I did some work for him once, and he's let me put one of my men on the elevator."

The car gained the open road and roared into high speed. Mason sat frowning thoughtfully until he had finished his cigarette. Then he pinched out the stub, dropped it in the ashtray, shook his head and said. "Somewhere along the line, Paul, I've overlooked the big bet in this case. It's just running around in circles."

"An inside tip from headquarters," Drake said, "is that they have enough on Rita Swaine to hang her. I don't want to discourage you on your case, Perry, but I thought you'd like to know."

Mason said, without taking his eyes from the road, his

profile grim and granite-hard, "Don't ever kid yourself, Paul, circumstantial evidence is sometimes a liar. I think this is one of the times."

"You don't think she did it?"

"No."

"Who did, then?"

"I'm damned if I know. I'm hoping there'll be something on the body of Jason Braun which will give us a clue as to whom he'd been talking with, where he's been hiding during the last day or two. He saw something in one of the windows. He must have told *someone* what he saw."

"Well, we'll know in a few minutes. We're eating up the miles now."

Again Mason sat back and was silent. Not until the car slued off to the side of the road where a light roadster was parked, with a man standing beside it frantically waving his arms, did the lawyer appear to be conscious of his surroundings. "That your man, Paul?" he asked then.

The detective nodded. "He'll lead the way," he said.

Mason sat forward on the edge of the seat, watching every curve in the road as it snaked its way up a precipitous canyon.

"What the devil was Jason Braun doing up here?" the lawyer asked.

"I can't figure it myself," Drake said, "unless he came up here to meet someone. Remember, he was an investigator working on a case, and—"

"And if he'd wanted complete privacy, he could have secured it just as well about twenty-five miles nearer the city," Mason interrupted.

Drake said, "We'll see."

The pilot car labored up the heavy grade, rounded a turn, and the stop light flashed an angry red of warning. Ahead of the car, a motorcycle officer, attired in whipcord, puttees and a leather coat, flagged the car to a stop. A tow car was parked crossways a hundred feet beyond him, a taut wire rope stretched down into the depths of the canyon. The motor of the car was turning slowly and the wire rope gradually reeling in over the revolving drums.

Mason and Drake jumped to the ground. Drake showed his card to the traffic officer. "I'm making an investigation of this," he said.

"What's the idea?" the officer wanted to know.

"I'm representing an insurance company," Drake said. "The big-shot thinks the man's a policy holder."

"What makes him think that?" the traffic officer wanted to know.

Drake shrugged his shoulders and said, "Probably just a poor hunch, but one of his policy holders has been missing for two or three days, and he's just playing it safe. Anyway, there's ten dollars a day and expenses in it for me, eight and expenses for the photographer, and this guy, here, so I should worry."

The traffic officer nodded. "I'd like prints of any pictures you take," he said.

"Sure," Drake told him.

"And don't mess up anything. The coroner hasn't arrived yet."

"Think he'll come?"

"He'll probably tell us to bring the body in, but we're awaiting definite instructions to make sure."

"Where's the body?" Mason asked.

"Over there under that tree, covered with a canvas. But you can't tell anything by that."

"Why not?"

"Take a look at the head and you'll see why. Lying out in the sun for a couple of days hasn't improved things any, either."

Drake said, "Okay, thanks, we'll take a look. Come on, boys, let's go."

They walked up the road to where the tow car, with its back wheels blocked, was straining at the weight on the other end of the steel line.

The sun beat down from a cloudless sky. The air in the canyon was dry, hot and still. A growth of scrub oak covered the slope which stretched down for a hundred feet below the roadbed to terminate abruptly in a fifty-foot drop. The tow car had raised the wreck above this drop and was now inching it up the slope. From time to time, branches of the scrub oak cracked explosively. Little spurts of powdery dust puffed upward from the trees.

Mason said to the man in charge of operations, "We're investigators," and moved over to the white canvas which had been spread beneath the shade of a big oak tree.

Picking up a corner of the canvas, he moved it back. Flies buzzed in angry circles. Mason dropped the canvas back into place and said, "Not much help there."

Drake dropped to his knees, brought out a small inked pad from his pocket and said, "I can get something from the finger-tips, Perry."

Mason once more turned a corner of the canvas back. The traffic officer continued to stand where he could warn traffic coming around the blind curve from below. The men in charge of raising the wreck from the canyon were completely occupied with the problems which confronted them. Someone shouted from down below. The winches ceased to turn, and the sounds of an ax, chopping away at a bush, could be heard from the thicket.

Drake transferred prints of the dead man's fingers to a white piece of paper, produced a magnifying glass and another set of prints from his pocket. Sitting on his heels beside the mangled form of the dead man, Drake made his comparison.

"Don't try to reduce it to a mathematical certainty," Mason said. "All I want is a working hypothesis."

"Well, you've got it," Drake told him. "This is the guy."

"Jason Braun?"

"Yes. Alias Packard."

There were shouts from the brush-covered slope. One of the men leaned over the edge of the road, steadying himself by holding to the wire cable. Mason said, "Okay, Paul, go through his pockets. I'll keep watch."

"It's highly irregular," Drake pointed out. "The coroner is the one who's supposed—"

"Forget it," Mason told him. "Go through his pockets. There's a car coming up the road now."

For a moment there was comparative silence in the canyon. The grinding winches of the big tow car had stopped. There were no more shouts from down below. The ax blows were suspended. In the hot silence could be heard the faint grind of a car coming up the winding road.

Drake nodded to his assistant. Turning back the canvas, they explored the stained, stiff clothes of the corpse.

Drake said, "A knife, some keys, a handkerchief, half-smoked package of cigarettes, card of matches from the Log Cabin Café in Pasadena, a pencil, fountain pen, forty-eight dollars in bills, two dollars and seven cents in small change. And that's all. No rings, stick pins, wrist watch—in fact, nothing else."

Mason said, "That car's about ready to come around the curve. Probably it's the coroner. Get that stuff back in his pockets. Make an inventory if you can."

The men pushed the things back in the pockets. Drake said, "Gosh, Perry, this is getting me where I live. I'm going to be sick."

"Shut up," Mason ordered. "Get busy and keep busy. I'll tell you when that car rounds the corner. Then get up and get away— Here it comes. Beat it!"

Drake's assistant jumped to his feet, pulled a cigarette from his pocket, inserted it in his lips and held the flame of a match cupped in trembling hands. Drake jerked the canvas back into position, took two uncertain steps toward Mason, veered abruptly, and leaned against the trunk of a tree. His face was a greenish-white.

The car slowed to a stop in front of the traffic officer's upraised palm. Two men got out. They talked for a few moments. Then the officer nodded and stood to one side.

Mason watched the two men.

"Is it the coroner?" Drake asked, without moving his position.

Mason said, "Move down toward that tow car, Paul, I'm joining you. Let's keep out of sight."

"Is it the coroner?" Drake repeated, still standing against the tree.

"It's Jimmy Driscoll and Rodney Cuff, his lawyer," Mason said. "Get going."

The three walked over to the tow car. The pair coming up the road walked with quick, jerky steps. Mason said, "Sort of circle around the hood, boys. Try to make everything you do seem casual. Don't look over toward them. Keep your eyes on the cable. Act as though we're part of the salvage crew."

Someone shouted from below. The man standing by the drums pushed on a lever, and the winches started slowly revolving.

Cuff and Driscoll walked to the edge of the road, peered down the taut line of the wire rope, then stepped back and walked directly to the canvas-covered figure.

Mason said, "Leave this to me, Paul. You fellows stay here."

He waited some thirty seconds, until Cuff had inserted his fingers in the pockets of the dead man's coat, then he casually walked forward and said, "I think the coroner likes to be the one to do that, Cuff."

Rodney Cuff jumped to his feet. Driscoll stared at Mason with the agonized expression of the landlubber who is about to be seasick.

Cuff's face was completely without expression, but, for a moment, there was a widening of the blue eyes. Then he grinned, stretched out his hand, "Well, well," he said, "fancy meeting you here!"

Mason took the outstretched hand, said, "You're interested in this case, Counselor?"

Cuff met his stare steadily. "All right," he said, "let's quit beating around the bush. Was this man Carl Packard, or wasn't he?"

"I never saw Carl Packard," Mason told him.

"There's ink on the fingers of his left hand," Cuff observed.

"What brought you out here?" Mason countered.

"I fancy," Cuff said, "that our mental processes were somewhat identical. Tell me, is it Packard?"

Mason met the younger man's eyes and said, "Yes, Cuff, it's Packard."

Cuff glanced over toward Jimmy Driscoll, then shifted his eyes quickly back to Mason. "Then," he said slowly, "we'll never know just what it was Packard saw in the window."

Mason turned to face Driscoll. "Don't be too sure about that, Cuff."

So far as he could ascertain, Driscoll's face didn't change expression by so much as the faintest flicker.

CHAPTER THIRTEEN

MASON gave his card to a sallow-faced woman in the late forties, who said, without even attempting a smile, "If you haven't an appointment with Mr. Dimmick I doubt if he'll see you. But be seated and I'll inquire."

Mason said, "Thanks," and remained standing.

She vanished through a door marked, "ABNER DIMMICK, *Private,*" and was gone for some thirty seconds. When she returned, she stood on the threshold, an angular figure, attired in a heavy woolen suit, deep-set, black eyes staring in lackluster scrutiny from behind horn-rimmed spectacles.

"Mr. Dimmick will see you," she said, and stood to one side for Mason to pass.

Mason closed the door behind him. Dimmick, seated back of a desk piled high with leather-backed law books, said, "How d'ye do, Counselor. Excuse me for not getting up. My rheumatism, you know. Sit down. What can I do for you—no, wait a minute."

He flipped up a lever on an inter-office loud-speaker and said to some person whose identity was not disclosed, "Tell Rodney Cuff to come in here right away."

Without waiting for any comment, he snapped the lever back into position, turned to Mason and said, "I want young Cuff to be here when we talk. He's handling this case."

Mason nodded, dropped into a chair, crossed his long legs in front of him and lit a cigarette. Dimmick regarded him through the haze of blue smoke and said, "How's your case coming?"

"So-so."

"I understand the police are holding back some evidence."

"That so?" Mason asked, raising his eyebrows.

Dimmick raised his bushy eyebrows, then lowered them into level lines of shrewd scrutiny, as he stared at Mason. "Damnedest thing I ever heard of," he said, "Dimmick, Gray & Peabody getting mixed up in a murder case! Can't seem to get accustomed to it. Wake up in the mornings with a start, feeling a sense of impending disaster, then realize it's just that damn murder case. I suppose you get accustomed to them."

"I do," Mason said.

"Going to have a fight on your hands to save Rita Swaine," Dimmick said. "Personally, I think it's a shame. Walter Prescott needed killing."

A door burst explosively open. Rodney Cuff, hurrying into the room, saw Mason, nodded, smiled, slowly closed the door behind him, and then, with every appearance of casual indifference, crossed over to the desk and said to Abner Dimmick, "You wanted me, Mr. Dimmick?"

"Yes. Sit down. Mr. Mason wants to say something. I thought he'd better talk with you, since you're handling the case."

"What I have to say," Mason said, taking the cigarette from his mouth and staring at the smoke which spiraled upward, "has to do with the Second Fidelity Savings & Loan."

"Indeed!" Dimmick said, raising his bushy eyebrows.

"You're attorneys for that institution," Mason said. "Walter Prescott kept an account there. I can't find out what's in that account, when the deposits were made, nor in what form they were made. In fact, I can't get a damn bit of information out of the bank."

Dimmick made clucking noises with his tongue against the roof of his mouth. "I asked you if you wanted to co-operate," he said at length. "You told me you didn't."

Cuff said, "Most embarrassing."

"It's going to be embarrassing for someone," Mason warned.

"Let's see," Cuff inquired, "has Mrs. Prescott been appointed administratrix?"

"She's filed a petition."

"Evidently she won't be charged with being an accessory," Cuff observed.

Mason said, "You're advising the bank. I want to know the facts about that account. I'm satisfied they're being withheld from me on the advice of counsel."

Dimmick started to get to his feet, fell back in his chair with a groan, said, "Now, Rodney, remember what the doctor said about my getting excited. *Don't* let me get excited!"

Cuff said, "Aren't you jumping to conclusions, Mr. Mason?"

"I think not," Mason told him, without taking his eyes from Dimmick.

"Well, after all," Dimmick said, "I haven't taken the time to look it up, but as I remember the law, until some person is actually appointed as executor or administrator, the bank doesn't have to answer questions."

"I'm not talking about what the law says right now," Mason said, "I'm telling you what I want."

"Of course," Dimmick pointed out, "we have to take the law into consideration in advising the bank."

Mason got to his feet. "You know my position," he said. "I'll expect to hear from the bank within an hour."

Dimmick pounded the floor with his cane. "You can't

get anything from us until Mrs. Prescott has been vin-
dicated or until she's been appointed by the court as
administratrix—"

Mason crossed the room to stand by the corner of the
older man's desk, looking down at him. "Dimmick," he
said slowly, "you live in an academic atmosphere of legal
abstraction. Your idea of rights and liabilities come from
reading the statutes. Now then, you've been dealt cards
in another sort of game entirely. You're not playing
auction bridge now, you're playing no-limit poker. Now,
you can co-operate with me, or not, just as you damn
please. If you *don't* co-operate with me on this matter,
I'm going to raise hell. I'll expect to hear from you within
an hour."

Dimmick struggled to his feet. "You look here," he
shouted, "you can't bulldoze us! You're not doing business with some cheap firm of shysters! Dimmick, Gray &
Peabody represent the—"

Mason said, "Don't forget what the doctor told you,
Mr. Dimmick. You mustn't get excited."

He strode toward the exit door, opened it, turned to
Cuff and said, "How about the wallet you took from
Packard's coat pocket, Cuff?"

"The wallet!" Cuff said, his eyes widening.

Mason nodded.

"There wasn't any wallet."

"There *isn't* any," Mason said. "That's no sign there
wasn't any."

"But I don't understand you," Cuff said. "You—"

"I understand him," Dimmick said. "He's going to *claim*
that you wrongfully removed a wallet from Packard's
pocket."

Mason said, "I'm not going to claim anything of the
sort, gentlemen. I *am* going to point out to the press that
it's most unusual for a man to be driving a car without a
driving license. When Dr. Wallace treated Packard at the
hospital, Packard had a driving license showing his name
and his Altaville residence. That driving license was in a

wallet. The wallet and the driving license were returned to him. What became of them?"

"How should I know?" Cuff asked.

"What were you doing, going through the man's pockets?"

"I was trying to identify him."

Mason nodded and said, "That's what *you* say. You're representing James Driscoll. Don't forget Prescott was killed with Driscoll's gun. Don't forget Carl Packard saw something in the window of Prescott's house just about the time Prescott was being killed. Don't forget that Packard was murdered to keep him from talking, and don't forget that James Driscoll knew that the body was that of Packard just as soon as the wreck was found. Perhaps the ultra-respectable firm of Dimmick, Gray & Peabody will have some embarrassing questions to answer before I get finished."

Cuff came striding toward Mason, his face indignant. "You can't pull that stuff," he said. "That's—"

"Good afternoon, gentlemen," Mason said, stepping into the corridor. "You have half an hour." He slammed the door shut behind him.

CHAPTER FOURTEEN

PERRY MASON, his thumbs pushed through the armholes of his vest, head dropped forward in thought, paced the floor of his office with rhythmic regularity. From time to time he flung remarks over his shoulder to Della Street; his eyes, however, kept staring straight ahead in fixed focus.

"—Can't understand the thing—like reaching in the dark for a light globe that's dangling from a string. It hits your fingers, bounces away. You grope for it, can't find it, then bump into it again. . . . What the devil *could* Packard have seen in that window? . . . And Packard was murdered, don't forget that. Personally, I'm inclined to think he was unconscious when somebody ran the car over the bank. In the first place, it was a stolen car. Now, why the devil should Packard steal a car? In the second place, there wasn't a single finger-print on the steering wheel, but Packard wasn't wearing gloves. Someone stole that car, wiped all prints from the steering wheel. Packard was unconscious. They ran the car up the mountain road, then someone who wore gloves stood on the runningboard, pushed down the hand throttle, kicked in the clutch, ran it to the edge of the cliff, and let 'er go."

Della Street tapped with her pencil on the polished surface of her desk. "Now listen, Chief," she said. "Don't forget our ship sails tomorrow. And, while I think of it, here's the ticket for you to sign."

She unfolded a sheet of paper filled with fine printing. Mason paused in his stride, whipped a fountain pen from his pocket, bent over the desk, and affixed his signature with a flourish.

"If a client did that you'd jump all over him," she said.

"Did what?"

"Sign a printed form without reading it."

He grinned. "*After* they get in trouble," he said, "and bring a printed document in to me, bearing their signature, I always tell them they shouldn't have signed it without reading it. And they shouldn't. Not *that* one. But if a business man stopped to read over the nine hundred and ninety-nine thousand fine print regulations they put on the backs of tickets, bills of lading, telegraph blanks, and things of that sort, he'd be blind before he was fifty."

"Perry Mason, you're avoiding the question. Are you or are you not going to start getting your trunks packed?"

He frowned and said, "You know as well as I do, Della, we can't leave on that ship until we have Rita Swaine out of her difficulties."

"Suppose she's guilty?"

"Do *you* think she's guilty?"

"To tell you the truth, Chief, I don't know. I don't think I pay as much attention to the sob-sister stories women hand out as you do. But, just the same, it's hard to figure how she could have gone in the house, killed Walter Prescott, and then tried to plan things so it would look as though her sister had done the job."

"How about Rosalind Prescott?"

"I'm not so sure about her. Rosalind's in love. A woman will do anything to protect the man she loves."

"Even to the extent of getting her sister convicted of murder!"

"Her sister isn't convicted of murder yet," Della Street pointed out. "And if she is, it'll be the first client you've defended who *has* been convicted. Rosalind may have passed the buck to you."

Mason resumed his pacing of the floor and said, "Yes, *that's* so."

"Chief, will you *please* take the time out tonight to pack your trunks?"

"I don't know," he said. "I can't promise. If I can't clear this case up, there's no use packing any trunks. You know as well as I do I won't sail unless it's finished."

"That isn't what's bothering me," she said. "I don't doubt your ability to work out a solution of *this* case before tomorrow afternoon at two o'clock. But, what I'm afraid of is, you'll get interested in some *other* case and stay over to handle that."

"No," he told her, "when we get this thing cleaned up we're going around the world."

"Will you promise you won't take on any other case?"

Mason said, with a grin, "Well, now, a promise is definite and final."

"So you really don't mean it."

"Well," he offered, "I'll make you a conditional promise."

"What do you mean by a conditional promise?"

"I won't take any ordinary case," he said. "Of course, if something should come in which fairly reeked of mystery — Well, you wouldn't want me to go around the world putting in every waking minute wondering what I'd left behind me, would you?"

"Yes," she said, "I would."

"I wouldn't enjoy the trip."

"You think you wouldn't. If you once got started you'd get a kick out of it. You'd see so much beneath the surface that you'd get a lot of fun sizing up your fellow travelers, going ashore in the different ports, and—"

She broke off, to lift the receiver from the telephone on her desk as the bell shrilled into noise. Listening a moment, she looked up and said, "Frederick Carpenter, the Vice-President of the Second Fidelity Savings & Loan."

Mason grinned and said, "That *may* be good. Better listen in."

He strode to his desk, jerked up his telephone, said, "Hello. Mason speaking."

"Good afternoon, Mr. Mason. This is Mr. Frederick Carpenter of the Second Fidelity Savings & Loan. You'll remember talking with me about the account of Walter Prescott, deceased."

"I remember it perfectly," Mason said, winking across at Della Street.

"At the time you talked with me," Carpenter went on, in the slow, deliberate voice of one who has trained himself not to do things in a hurry, "I felt that it would be far better to wait until your client had been appointed by the court before making any accounting. However, after taking the matter up with our legal department, we have concluded that perhaps it might be better to co-operate with you and not force you to take steps to ascertain the exact amount which—"

Mason impatiently interrupted the smooth cadences of the banker's voice. "Never mind explaining," he said. "How much is his balance?"

Carpenter cleared his throat. "Sixty-nine thousand, seven hundred and sixty-five dollars and thirty cents," he said.

"Can you tell me how that's been deposited?"

"The deposits," Carpenter said, "were rather unusual.

For the most part, they represented sums ranging from five to fifteen thousand dollars, deposited in cash."

"By Walter Prescott personally?"

"As far as I am able to ascertain from our records and the recollection of the persons who handled the account, by Walter Prescott personally."

"Thanks," Mason said.

"And if we can be of any assistance to you in the future," Carpenter said, "please ask for me personally, Mr. Mason."

Mason said, "Okay," dropped the receiver into place, and stared across at Della Street. "That," he said, "doesn't look very much as though we were sailing tomorrow."

"Why not, Chief?"

"It means there's another complicating circumstance which we haven't considered; something which has to be ironed out before we can reach a solution."

"Why does it have to be ironed out?"

"Because," he told her, "a solution of any crime which doesn't account for all of the various factors involved is no solution at all. Now, I've paid too much attention to the people the district attorney's office suspect, and not enough to the victim. In the long run, Della, the essence of all successful detective work lies in reconstructing the life of the victim. That gives motivation, and motivation makes murders.

"Virtually every man has enemies. Sometimes they're business enemies. More often they're personal enemies, people who hate him, people who will look down their noses and say it's too bad when they hear he's bumped off, but who will be tickled to death just the same; but it takes a peculiar psychological build-up to perpetrate a murder. A man must have a certain innate ferocity, a certain lack of consideration, and, usually, a lack of imagination."

"Why a lack of imagination?"

"I don't know," he said, "except that it's nearly always true. I think imaginative people sympathize with the sufferings of others because they're able to visualize those sufferings more keenly in their own minds. An unimaginative person, on the other hand, can't visualize himself in the shoes of another. Therefore, he sees life only from his own selfish angle. Killers are frequently cunning, but they're rarely original. They're selfish, and usually determined. Of course, I'm not talking now about a murder which is the result of some sudden overpowering emotion."

"Why couldn't this murder be one of that type?" she asked.

"It could," he admitted readily enough. "In that event, I'd say that Rita Swaine pulled the trigger. But, whether she was justified, is another question."

"Would you represent her if she's guilty?"

"It depends on what you mean by being guilty. I don't necessarily define murder the same way the district attorney defines it. If there were circumstances of moral provocation, they might be just as compelling as circumstances of physical provocation. In other words, the law says that if a man is in a position to do you great bodily harm, or to kill you, and he comes at you, apparently for the purpose of putting a murderous intent into execution, you have the right to kill him. In other words, that's a physical provocation. It's all the law, in its blundering generality, can take into comprehension. But, how about the person who brings a crushing mental or moral pressure upon a more or less helpless victim? I admit circumstances like that aren't common. But, with certain temperaments, they might be possible."

"Chief," she said, "will you *please* unfocus your mind long enough to get your clothes packed?"

"Not now," he told her, frowning, and starting once more to pace the floor. "I'm going back to first principles and building up from there. Now then, let's look at the victim—Walter Prescott—an unsocial individual—selfish, cruel, cold, ruthless— In short, just the type of person who could commit a murder."

"But he didn't commit a murder, Chief. He was murdered."

Mason said, "That's the puzzling part of it, Della. He should have been the murderer instead of the corpse."

"This," Della Street pointed out, "isn't getting us any nearer China."

"I think it is," Mason said thoughtfully. "It sounds foolish, and yet I think it's getting me some place. It's paradoxical. The man who was murdered isn't the man who was murdered, but the man who committed the murder. Now, if we can follow that contradictory premise through to a logical conclusion, Della, we're certainly going to be one jump ahead of the police, because that's a starting point of deductive reasoning which would never suggest itself to them."

"No," she admitted with a smile, "you win on that."

"Now then," Mason said, "let's suppose that Walter Prescott is a murderer. Let's suppose that what Jason Braun, alias Carl Packard, saw in the window of that house didn't have to do with the murder of Walter Prescott but did have to do with the murder of someone else —someone Walter Prescott was killing."

Della Street said, "You also win on that, Chief. I can't conceive of the police being able to follow you into *that* line of reasoning."

"It's goofy," he admitted, "and yet, somehow or other, I feel that I'm getting on the track of what really happened. Somehow, putting all these possibilities in words takes away that feeling of fumbling around in the dark. Now then, with that as a starting point, and considering that Packard saw something connected with a murder, who was the victim? If Walter Prescott had killed someone, who would he have killed? If he'd *tried* to kill someone, who was that someone, and what could Packard have seen— Wait a minute, Della—good Lord!"

Mason paused in his pacing, to stand in the middle of the floor, his legs spread apart. "Della," he said slowly, "if what *I* think happened is actually the real solution, then—"

A series of knocks sounded on the door which led

to the corridor. Mason said, "That's Paul Drake. Let him in, Della, and see what he wants."

Della Street crossed the room and opened the door.

"Hello, folks," Drake said. "What're you doing?"

"We're engaging in a new form of logic," Della answered with a grin. "It's swell. It solves murders and everything."

"Gimme," Drake said, entering the room.

"Well, it goes like this," Della said. "Because you've come in the room, you must have been the person going out of the room. Therefore, having gone out of the room while you were coming into the room, someone who saw you in the corridor coming into the room, would have known you were going out of the room, and—"

"Oh, I see," Drake said, "like a puppy chasing his tail, huh?"

"Exactly," Della agreed, "only the puppy catches his tail. Then, having swallowed himself, he becomes, so to speak, completely self-contained."

Mason chuckled and said, "Don't mind her, Paul. She's filled with travel bugs. She's been down picking out light whatnots to wear in tropical countries."

"Not only in the countries," Della Street said, "but on shipboard, under the stars, and in the moonlight. Think, Chief, of sailing down below the equator, with the Southern Cross blazing overhead, the wind a warm caress on the skin, the wake of the boat streaming out behind in a white path. The scent of spices in the air, the hiss of water past the bow. Over on the right—"

"Starboard," Drake interrupted. "By the time you've gone below the equator, you'll know the nautical terms."

"Okay," she said, with a sweep of her arm, "over on the starboard is an island, the crests of the volcanic mountains silhouetted against the stars. Down lower against the water, where the palm trees fringe the lagoon behind the barrier reef, is a native village. And, from the deck of the ship you can hear the rhythmic throb of the native drums, the peculiar wail of primitive music—"

"No," Mason interrupted, "you're wrong again. The

captain wouldn't be standing in that close to an island after dark. He'd be out where there was plenty of sea room and—"

Della Street shook her head sadly. "Pardon me! My mistake! What we should talk about is murder—corpses with battered heads—clues, circumstantial evidence, blood-stained bullets, perjured testimony, and the beautiful things in life. Murderers who are corpses, corpses who are murderers. Now you, Paul Drake, get a load of this: Tomorrow the Chief and I are going to sail on the *President Monroe* on a round-the-world cruise. We have our state-rooms all engaged, our tickets bought and paid for. There's only one thing standing between us and the gangplank and that's this Rita Swaine, who drifted in here with a lame canary and a hard luck story and got the Chief all tangled up in a mess. Now, you two get busy and straighten it out. But just remember that tomorrow—"

Drake, who had slid into his favorite position in the big leather chair, shook his head mournfully and said, "That's what I came to tell you about, Perry. It's all over except the shouting. You can sail any time you get ready."

"What's happened?" Mason asked.

"Your client's confessed."

"You mean Rita?"

"Yes."

"What did she confess to?"

"Oh, a lot of things—going upstairs to change her clothes, stepping into the bedroom, finding Walter's body, going through his pockets, taking a letter out of his wallet, and all that sort of stuff. After the contradictory stories she's told, plus the fact that she forthwith skipped out of the state and fought extradition, a jury will bring in a first-degree murder verdict without leaving the box. You can probably get her life imprisonment if you change her plea from not guilty to guilty, and right now that's the best thing you can do for your client. Then you can catch your ship and go bye-bye."

Mason stood staring down at the detective. "How did you hear about this, Paul?"

"One of the newspaper boys tipped me off. The district attorney released a statement. The thing will be on the street in half an hour. Hell, Perry, they had the goods on her, anyway. They had her fingerprints on the wallet, and they've found bloodstains on her shoes and had reconstructed enough of the charred fragments in the fireplace to know what letter had been taken from Prescott's pocket and burned. The D.A. was holding all that stuff back, getting ready to slap you in the face with it when you walked into court."

"Did she," Mason asked, "admit that she killed him?"

"I don't know. I think she's still holding out on that."

"Anything else?" Mason asked. "What have you found out about that Rosa Hendrix?"

Drake said, "Hell, Perry, you know the answer to that without me having to tell you. If you want to be mean about it, you'll have a chance to do it tonight."

"How so?"

"She's leaving for Reno tonight."

"You mean Rosa Hendrix?"

"No, not Rosa Hendrix, but Diana Morgan, the rich young divorcee who has the swell apartment in the Bellefontaine."

"Certain about that?" Mason asked.

"Yes."

"Okay. What else?"

"Something's happened to whatever it was Trader delivered to the garage. He says he can't remember exactly, a couple of boxes, and he thinks a barrel. At any rate, the stuff disappeared. Trader says he set it just inside the door, as Prescott had instructed him to."

"Perhaps the D.A. took it for evidence," Mason said.

"No. One of the newspaper boys did a little snooping for me and finds out that the district attorney overlooked that angle of the case entirely."

"I wonder," Mason said thoughtfully, "if the whole thing may not have been a stall. I'm wondering if Trader actually did return to Prescott's house and deliver stuff to the garage."

"Yes. Mrs. Weyman saw him back the van up to the garage."

"How about Weyman? Was he home at the time?"

"He was home, but indisposed," Drake grinned.

Mason looked at his wrist watch. "What else do you have on Rosa Hendrix, anything?"

"Not a thing," Drake said cheerfully. "Rosa Hendrix is a nice girl, but I have my suspicions about Diana Morgan. That girl seems to know her way around and she has an independent income from some place."

"How about Wray?" Mason asked. "Does he play around with the redhead after office hours?"

"Apparently not. Wray is quite a mixer, fond of clubs, lodges, smokers and all that sort of stuff. His gregarious instinct seems to have for its ultimate goal the making of contracts and the landing of business for the firm of Prescott & Wray."

"Any idea who's putting up the money?" Mason asked.

"Not for Diana Morgan," Drake said, "but I have a line on Rosa Hendrix."

"What sort of a line?"

"In case you're interested," Drake said, "she has a luncheon engagement tomorrow with Jimmy Driscoll."

Mason stared at him with thought-slitted eyes.

"Listen, Paul," he said, "what sort of baggage does that woman have?"

"Rosa Hendrix," Drake said, "has a cheap, split-leather suitcase with a pasteboard backing, a steamer trunk, and—"

"No, I'm not talking about *her*. I'm talking about her other identity—Diana Morgan."

"The sort of baggage that would go well with a three-hundred-and-ninety-five dollar apartment," Drake said. "Hat boxes, suitcases, trunks, finest of leather—"

"How are they marked?"

"Simply with the initials 'D.M.' You'll have a chance to see the stuff tonight, Perry. She'll be moving out on that trip to Reno."

"Do you think she actually intends to go to Reno?"

"Diana Morgan does," Drake said, grinning, "but Rosa Hendrix will be on the job tomorrow—don't forget Rosa's luncheon engagement with Jimmy Driscoll."

"I won't," Mason promised him. "Do you happen to know what time tonight she intends to move the baggage, Paul?"

" 'Happen' is not the word to describe the manner in which I attain my knowledge," Drake said, twisting his fish-mouth into a droll grin. "It takes elbow-grease, concentration, perspicacity, and perspiration, a rare combination of intuitive—"

"Yes, I know," Mason interrupted, matching his grin. "I'll find all that in the expense account when I get it. But, please tell me, Mr. Worldly-Wise Man, what time she intends to move the baggage."

"She told the porter to be up at her apartment at ten-thirty; that a transfer man would be waiting outside the apartment house at that time."

Mason said, "And do you *happen* to know, Mr. Human Wonder, whether the transfer man who will move the baggage of Miss Diana Morgan is Mr. Harry Trader of the Trader's Transfer Company?"

The grin left Paul Drake's face. His round, slightly protruding eyes showed a flash of surprise back of the glassy film which covered them. He slid around in the chair, got to his feet and said, "By God, Perry, I don't. And I'm going to find out. You hit the nail on the finger with *that* crack."

"Let me know as soon as you get the dope," Mason called out as Drake jerked open the exit door and pounded down the corridor toward the office.

Mason turned to Della Street. "Della, how about *your* baggage?"

"I have my things nearly all packed."

"I'm not talking about your things," he told her. "How about your baggage?"

"You mean my suitcases, trunks and things?"

"Yes."

"Oh," she said, "I'll get by. I've borrowed a couple of trunks and—"

"I have an idea which beats that all to pieces," Mason interrupted. "Why not let Rita Swaine pay for your baggage? I have a scheme by which—"

"Now listen, Chief," she interrupted. "*I'm* going to catch that boat. If you're thinking up any stunt which'll land me in jail you can forget it right now."

"No," he told her, "this'll be perfectly legal."

"Never mind if it's legal," she said. "Will it *look* legal?"

"Well," Mason admitted, hesitating, "I'll confess that it may *look* just the slightest bit—"

She interrupted and said, "That's enough. The answer, in words of one syllable is 'No.' "

"Now don't be like that, Della," he pleaded. "This is a cinch. You go down to the best luggage store in the city, buy yourself a whole flock of suitcases, hat boxes, trunks and what have you, and have them lettered with the initials 'D.M.' You put in some bricks, newspapers, boards and old shoes, to give the luggage a reasonable amount of weight. Then you have a transfer man take the luggage up to Rita Swaine's apartment at 1388 Chestnut Street. Tell him the number of the apartment is 408, and if you're not there he's to get a passkey from the attendant and put the baggage right in the apartment."

Della Street yawned and said, "Sorry, Chief, I'm not interested. When the ship pulls out tomorrow, I want to be standing on deck, waving bye-bye to a few of my envious friends who'll have come down to see me off. I wouldn't care to be behind bars in the county jail, thank you."

"You don't have to be," Mason told her. "This is perfectly legal."

"Will I get arrested?"

"They can't hold you in jail—"

"Never mind whether they can *hold* me. Will they arrest me?"

"Well," Mason conceded, "before we get done Sergeant Holcomb may be a little bit put out about it."

"Enough so he'd take me to the hoosegow, Chief?"

Mason said, "Sergeant Holcomb's impulsive, but I'll tell you what we'll do. We'll steal a march on him, Della. Get your book and I'll give you some dictation."

She said, "Oh, well, you've never yet gone so far I wouldn't back your play. Let's go."

She moved over to her secretarial desk, opened her shorthand notebook and held her pen poised above the paper, "Okay, Chief," she said, "what is it?"

"In the Matter of the Application of Della Street," Mason dictated, "for a Writ of *Habeas Corpus*."

CHAPTER FIFTEEN

LOW-FLUNG CLOUDS, borne along in solemn procession by a brisk south wind, slid smoothly over the city streets, sending down an occasional patter of raindrops. The morning was depressing, gloomy, a fore-runner of disaster.

The transfer man who stood awkwardly ill at ease in front of the apartment house desk, said, "Well, all I know about it is she *said* she was moving in. She had a sub-lease or something. She said all the baggage initialed 'D.M.' was to go in. Here, she said to give you this letter if I had any trouble."

The clerk said, "Well, you're having trouble," and slit open the envelope. He read the document, scratched his head and said, "Well, it seems to be in order. Rita Swaine has her rent paid and she's in jail. She says to let a Miss Della Street move her things into the apartment, and these are Della Street's things. I guess she has the right to do it if she wants. I'll send the boy up to unlock the door."

The transfer man nodded, walked back to the light transfer wagon at the curb, and started unpiling bags, suitcases and steamer trunks.

"How you going to get all that stuff into the one apartment?" the clerk asked.

"I d'know," the transfer man admitted. "I'll do it some way. Pile 'em in the center of the floor if I can't do nothing else. She said to get 'em in, and I'll get 'em in."

The colored elevator boy approached the desk. "Boss, yo'-all remembah that the police officer man said you was to telephone him if anybody tried to get in that apartment."

"No one's trying to get in," the clerk said. "The man's simply delivering some baggage. However, I'll notify Sergeant Holcomb."

He plugged in a line, called police headquarters and asked for Sergeant Holcomb of the homicide squad. While he waited, the transfer man and the elevator boy moved baggage up to Rita Swaine's apartment.

After a few moments Sergeant Holcomb's voice said, "Hello. What is it?"

"This is the desk clerk at 1388 Chestnut Street. You'll remember Miss Rita Swaine has an apartment here under lease, and you asked me to let you know if anyone tried to move anything out. Well, no one's trying to take anything out, but some baggage is being delivered—that is, Miss Swaine has given orders to place Miss Street's baggage in her apartment. The transfer man's brought quite a few suitcases, trunks and— Just a minute, I'll look— Yes, that's right, it's Della Street— What?— Well, I'll be damned!"

The clerk pulled out the plug and set his face in stern lines of officious determination.

Della Street, tailored to the minute, as serenely confident as a poker player pushing a stack of blue chips into the center of the pile, came breezing in from the street door walked up to the desk and said, "I'm Miss Street. I've made a terrible mistake."

"You're the one who sent the baggage for Miss Swaine's apartment?" the clerk asked.

"That's right. But this baggage shouldn't have gone up there at all. This is the 'D.M.' baggage. It should have been delivered to the Trader's Transfer Company for storage. Where's the transfer man, please?"

"He's upstairs now."

"Yes. I saw the truck out in front," Della Street said, as she dazzled the clerk with a smile, walked over to the elevator and jabbed the elevator button.

The elevator took her to the fourth floor. The desk clerk, hesitating for a moment, once more plugged in the line and said, "Police Headquarters." Again he asked to talk with Sergeant Holcomb, and, after a two minute delay, was advised that Holcomb had just left.

The clerk was pulling out the plug when the elevator door once more opened, an a perspiring transfer man started pitching out suitcases, hat boxes, trunks, and hand bags. The elevator made two trips of it. Della Street came down with the second load, trim, alert, and smiling. She said to the desk clerk, "Thank you very much indeed," and walked to the door of the apartment house. The eyes of the desk clerk followed her with ardent masculine appreciation.

Less than five minutes later, Sergeant Holcomb came striding into the lobby. "Where is she?" he asked.

The clerk waved a deprecating hand. "It's all right, Sergeant. I'm sorry I bothered you. I tried to get you again. It was all a mistake, but it's all right now."

"What the hell do you mean, it's all right now?"

"She's left."

"Who's left?"

"Della Street."

"She was here?"

"Yes."

"How about the baggage? Did you put that in the room?"

"No. She changed her mind, said that there'd been a mistake. So there's nothing to bother about. She took it with her."

"She what!"

"Took it with her."

"You opened up the room with a passkey?"

"I didn't personally. The elevator operator did."

"And put that baggage in?"

"No," the clerk said, "that's what I've been trying to tell you, Sergeant. The baggage didn't go in. It was a mistake. As soon as I saw Miss Street, I realized it must have been—"

"Never mind that," Sergeant Holcomb interrupted, pushing his face across the counter. "Did that baggage go in that room—even for a second?"

"Oh, well, if you want to put it that way, I don't know. I suppose some of it may have actually entered the room for a second or two. I wasn't there.

"Was Della Street alone in the room with any of that baggage?"

"Why, I wouldn't know—wait a minute, let me see— Yes, she must have been, because the first load of baggage came down with the operator and the transfer man in the cage. They unloaded that bunch of baggage and went back for another bunch. Miss Street must have been in the room with—"

"You fool!" Holcomb yelled. "She's Perry Mason's secretary. Perry Mason's defending Rita Swaine. They wanted something out of that room and didn't know how else to get it, so she took that baggage *in*, manipulated things so she was left alone in the room, opened one of the empty suitcases, pitched whatever it was she wanted in there, and took it out."

The clerk stared at Sergeant Holcomb with shocked, incredulous eyes. At length he said, "Why, Sergeant, she's a perfect little lady, trim, well-tailored, refined—"

"Bah!" Sergeant Holcomb said. "You make me sick. Why the hell didn't you hold her?"

"Hold her? How could I?"

"Tell her she was under arrest. Hold her until I got there."

"But you told me particularly, Sergeant, not to tell anyone you were coming."

Sergeant Holcomb's face darkened, as he groped for words. Suddenly the clerk had a bright idea.

"But wait a minute, Sergeant. I can tell you *where* she's taking the baggage. If you hurry, you can catch it there."

"Where?"

"The Traders's Transfer Company. They're going to store it."

"What does it look like?"

"Well, it's a very good grade of baggage, looks rather new. Very fine leather and—"

"What does it consist of?"

"Oh, everything. Hat boxes, hand bags, Gladstones, suitcases, steamer trunks—"

"Any identifying marks?"

"Yes. They're all lettered 'D.M.' "

" 'D.M.'?"

"Yes."

"Her name's Della Street. Why should she have D.M. on her baggage?"

"I don't know, I'm sure. I'm just describing the baggage to you. She said something about the D.M. baggage being the wrong baggage. If you want to examine it, you can probably intercept it if—"

Sergeant Holcomb whirled and crossed the lobby at a run. A moment later the clerk heard the scream of a siren.

Emil Scanlon looked across the coroner's jury and said, "You gentlemen have seen the remains."

They nodded.

"The object of this inquest is to determine how that man met his death," Scanlon said. "It may have been an accidental death, or it may have been something else. There's even a possibility of suicide. I want you gentlemen to pay close attention to the evidence. This isn't like a court of law. I conduct my inquests more or less informally. What I'm trying to do is to get at the facts. Some coroners don't care to have attorneys asking questions. Sometimes I don't. But, in a case of this sort, where I feel attorneys aren't getting technical and taking up time, but are actually assisting us in getting somewhere, I'm always glad to allow questions. I think you gentlemen understand your duties. We'll call the first witness."

There was a commotion in the courtroom. A man, whose face was so completely bandaged that only a bit of his nose and one eye were visible, said in muffled tones, "I want to be excused."

"Who are you?" Scanlon asked.

"I'm Jackson Weyman. I was a witness in that other inquest, and now somebody's subpoenaed me for this inquest. I'm a sick man."

"What's the matter with you?"

"Cuts in my face got infected," Weyman explained. "I have no business to be out. I should be home in bed right now and—"

He was interrupted by a thin, austere woman who stood up at the other end of the courtroom and said, "The same is true in *my* case, your Honor. I'm Mrs. Stella Anderson. I also was a witness in that other case. I've been ordered to appear in this case and testify. I know absolutely nothing about this young man—"

"Perhaps you two know more than you think you do," Scanlon said. "Since you're here under subpoena, I'll ask you to sit down and listen to at least a few of the witnesses. And, as far as you're concerned, Mr. Weyman, on account of your physical condition, I'll call you just as soon as I can. The first witness, however, will be Dr. James Wallace."

Dr. Wallace arose and walked toward the witness chair.

"But I demand that something be done about letting me go," Weyman said, his words somewhat muffled by his bandages. "I have an infection which may be dangerous unless I keep absolutely quiet and—"

"You should have produced a physician's certificate," Scanlon said. "Since you're here, simply sit down and compose yourself. I'll finish with you in a very few minutes. I have only a few routine questions to ask of Dr. Wallace.

"Dr. Wallace, you're a duly qualified and practicing physician and surgeon in this state and a resident physician and head of the interns at the Good Samaritan Hospital in this city. Is that right?"

"Yes, sir."

"And you have been for more than a year?"

"That's right."

"Now, you've seen the remains in the undertaking parlors?"

"I have."

"Do you know that man?"

"Yes," Dr. Wallace said slowly. "I do. That man is an individual whom I treated for shock, for minor abrasions, bruises, and for traumatic amnesia on the thirteenth of this month."

"Where, Doctor?"

"At the Good Samaritan Hospital. He had, I understand, been the victim of an automobile accident. He regained consciousness as he was being brought into the hospital. I found that his physical injuries were relatively superficial, treated them, and, in the course of my conversation, discovered that the man was suffering from traumatic amnesia. He—"

"Just what do you mean by traumatic amnesia, Doctor?"

"A loss of memory superinduced by external violence. He didn't know who he was, nor where he lived."

"So what did you do, Doctor?"

"Very adroitly," Dr. Wallace said, "I maneuvered the conversation around so that it included the city of Altaville. I had previously ascertained from a driving license found in his pocket that the man was a resident of Altaville, and that his name was Carl Packard. By leading the conversation to Altaville and its environments in such a way that I did not add to his mental shock, I soon cleared up the patient's mental condition."

"What did you do with the driving license?"

"I returned it to him."

"And he knew who he was at that time?"

"Oh, yes, he remembered his identity and was able to discuss matters intelligently."

"Now, Doctor, after leaving the hospital, this man disappeared."

"So I am given to understand."

"He was next found pinned under a wrecked automobile at the bottom of a precipitous canyon in the Santa Monica Mountains. The very severe injuries he had sustained had evidently killed him almost instantly, as will be shown by the testimony of the autopsy surgeon."

"Yes," Dr. Wallace said, "I noticed in making even a superficial examination that the skull had been completely crushed."

"There were also numerous other internal injuries and broken bones. Now, Doctor, I want to know if it's possible that the patient wasn't cured of this amnesia that you mentioned, but was wandering around in sort of a daze."

"Absolutely not," Dr. Wallace said positively, and somewhat belligerently. "When I discharge a patient as cured, he's cured. If there had been any possibility of an immediate recurrence of this condition, I would not have discharged him. Of course, you'll understand, however, if there'd been some *independent* shock, some other injury, perhaps, it is possible that another and separate traumatic amnesia might have developed, but it would have been *entirely* separate and distinct. Of course, there's nothing except the law of averages which prevents a man who has been run over by an automobile and treated by me going out and immediately becoming involved in another automobile accident. Yet they are separate and distinct accidents."

"We understand that," Scanlon said. "Now, what can you tell us about the identification you have made?"

"Well, in view of the condition of the cadaver," Dr. Wallace observed, "my identification must, of course, be predicated upon certain matters of circumstantial evidence. For instance, it has been definitely established that the man who gave me the name of Carl Packard at the hospital, and who apparently lived in Altaville, was, in reality, an investigator for the Board of Fire Underwriters, named Jason Braun. He had apparently taken the alias of Carl

Packard for the purpose of facilitating some of his investigations, and, having recovered his memory as to his alias, he naturally remembered his reason for concealing his true identity. Which is why he never once mentioned the name of Jason Braun to me, but agreed with me in the assumption he was Carl Packard of Altaville.

"Now, the Board of Fire Underwriters has its investigators all fingerprinted and, despite the partial decomposition of the cadaver, the ridges and whorls of the fingers can be readily ascertained. While I am not a fingerprint expert, I am an anatomist and I have carefully compared the fingerprints of the cadaver with those of Jason Braun. Having first assured myself that the man whom I treated was in reality Jason Braun, I have no hesitancy in identifying that man as being one and the same person with the cadaver lying at present in the undertaking parlors adjoining this room."

"I think that's all, Dr. Wallace," Scanlon said.

"Just a moment," Perry Mason observed. "Might I have the indulgence of the coroner in asking one or two questions?"

The coroner nodded.

"At the time this man, Packard, or Braun, whichever you wish to call him, recovered consciousness at the hospital—that is, when he recovered his knowledge of his identity—did he discuss the accident with you, Doctor?"

"He did."

"What did he say about it?"

"He said that he had seen something in the window of a house on his right which had caused him to focus all of his attention on that window and he neglected to look where he was going; that suddenly he realized some huge bulk was towering on his left. He swung his eyes back to the road in time to see this big moving van just about to make a turn into Fourteenth Street. He tried to apply his brakes, but by that time it was too late. The moving van hit him and the two cars swung into the curb where Packard lost consciousness at the moment of impact."

Rodney Cuff, on his feet, said suavely, "If the coroner

please, I object to this form of inquiry. This man, Braun, or Packard, as the case may be, is now dead. He can never testify in any trial as to *what* he saw. Any attempt to perpetuate his testimony in the records by this indirect method is highly irregular, and calls for hearsay and a conclusion of the witness."

"No, it doesn't," Scanlon said. "We're trying to determine how this man met his death, whether he was murdered, whether he committed suicide, or whether he was driving a car in a sort of daze and went off the side of the mountain."

"May it be understood, then, that this is the only purpose for which this evidence is admitted?" Cuff said. "That it's not binding upon anyone in any other matter, and—"

"I think that's the law anyway," Scanlon pointed out. "However, we're only trying to determine what caused this man to meet his death. And, so far as I know, *at the present time*, Mr. Cuff, there's no charge against your client implicating him in any way with *this* death."

"I resent that remark," Cuff said quickly. "You are intimating that before the inquest is concluded evidence *will* indicate that my client, Mr. Driscoll, had something to do with the death."

"I made no such implication," the coroner said, "and as far as I'm concerned, you're out of order and aren't helping the rights of your client any. Sit down."

Cuff started to say something, then changed his mind, and slowly sat down.

"Any further questions of the doctor?" Scanlon asked Perry Mason.

"I think that's all," Perry Mason said.

"Does the district attorney's office wish to interrogate Dr. Wallace?" Scanlon inquired.

Overmeyer shook his head and said, "Not at present, anyway. We wish to interrogate the autopsy surgeon and the traffic officers who discovered the body— Just a moment, there is *one* question. Dr. Wallace, this man didn't tell you anything at all which would indicate what he had seen in that window, did he?"

"He did not, beyond saying that it was something very startling or compelling, or something of that sort. I can't recall his *exact* words. I remember that he seemed rather sheepish about it."

"That's all."

Dr. Wallace walked down the aisle of the room which was being used for the inquest. Perry Mason said suddenly, "Just a moment, Doctor, I'd like to have you remain here for a few minutes. I don't think it will be over five or ten minutes at the most. Would you mind taking that seat?"

Mason indicated a seat on the aisle which had been occupied but a moment before by Jackson, his law clerk. That seat was now vacant, and Dr. Wallace, frowning, looked at his wrist watch, said, "Very well, but I have some important cases at the hospital and would like to be released as soon as possible."

"You will be, Doctor," Scanlon said. "Just be seated for a moment."

Dr. Wallace dropped into the chair. Jackson Weyman, who occupied the adjoining seat, turned the one eye visible through his bandages to stare curiously at the doctor.

"The next witness," Coroner Scanlon announced, "will be Edward Bird, one of the traffic officers who came on the body at the scene of the accident."

Edward Bird, advancing to be sworn, apparently enjoying the interest he aroused, stood very erect as he faced the jury, and made certain that the coat of his uniform was snugly fitting and unwrinkled. He adjusted the gun which hung at his hip from the wide brown belt, sat down, turned to the coroner and said, "Yes, sir."

"You are one of the officers who discovered the body of this man who is at present lying in the undertaking parlors?"

"Yes, sir, I and my partner, Jack Moore, were cruising up this road, making a cut-off from the ocean boulevard to get over to the Conejo route, when I happened to notice that some branches had been freshly broken from one of the scrub oaks just down the hill from the edge of the road. We stopped the car, investigated, and found where some heavy object had crashed down through the trees. We worked our way down the ledge, and then came to an abrupt drop of about sixty or seventy feet. We could see a car lying upside-down in the bottom of this canyon. It took us almost half an hour to work our way down to it. This man was pinned underneath the car. The top had caved in, and the back of the front seat had crushed his head like an egg shell. He had been dead for some time. The body already showed evidences of decomposition. It had been lying for two days in the hot sun."

"What did you do?"

"We notified the coroner, obtained a wrecking outfit, first raised the body to the road, and then brought up the machine."

"Were you present when representatives of the district attorney's office tested the steering wheel of the automobile for fingerprints?"

"I was."

"What did they find?"

"There were no fingerprints on the steering wheel."

"Were you present when the pockets of the dead man's clothes were emptied?"

"I was."

"I show you an assortment of articles and ask you if you can identify them," the coroner said. He took from his safe a black leather hand bag, took from this hand bag a towel and spread out a miscellaneous assortment. The officer checked them over carefully, nodded his head, and said, "Yes, these were the things which were in the pockets of the dead man's clothes. There was nothing else in the clothes."

"You're certain of that?"

"Yes."

"Now, what can you tell us of the automobile which was lying there, wrecked, in the bottom of the canyon?"

"It was a stolen automobile. It had been stolen at six-thirty on the afternoon of the thirteenth; was reported about an hour later, and wasn't seen again until it was found in the bottom of this canyon."

"I think that's all," the coroner said. "Are there any questions?"

Mason slowly got to his feet.

"You have some questions, Mr. Mason?"

Mason said, "I have some questions to ask of this witness. But, in the meantime, I am wondering if the coroner has forgotten his promise to Mr. Weyman. Mr. Weyman is evidently a very sick man and I think that he should be put on the stand at the present time, if he is to be called at all. In fact, I think the evidence in this case is very plain, and it seems to me there is no reason to call Mr. Weyman. I suggest that Mr. Weyman be excused."

"No," the coroner said, "Mr. Weyman is here, and there's no reason why he can't testify."

"But he's a sick man," Mason insisted.

"He hasn't a physician's certificate to prove it," the coroner pointed out. "If he was too sick to attend, he could have had his physician certify to that fact."

"Well, it's very evident he's ill," Mason said. "Look at the man's bandaged countenance. He certainly wouldn't go around with his face swathed like that unless he was ill—here, I have a suggestion. There's a doctor sitting right next to him. Let Dr. Wallace make an examination of the infected area and give a certificate. *I* don't think a man in that condition should be a witness."

Dr. Wallace looked questioningly at the coroner. The coroner stared steadily at Perry Mason. Then Scanlon said, "Very well, Doctor, you make an examination."

Dr. Wallace reached over, deftly tore off a strip of adhesive tape, took one end of the bandage in his fingers, and started to untwist it.

Weyman swung his left fist. The blow caught Dr. Wallace full on the jaw, snapping his head back. But the doctor's fingers still held the end of the bandage.

Weyman started climbing over the back of the seat. The coroner yelled, "Stop that man!" and someone grabbed

his legs. Weyman kicked out desperately. Dr. Wallace, recovering himself somewhat, grabbed at the collar of the man's coat with his left hand. His right pulled at the bandage. Suddenly, the entire bandage slid from Weyman's face, to lump around his neck, and Dr. Wallace, staring at the man's features, jumped back to stare with wide, startled eyes. "Good God!" he exclaimed.
"That's the dead man!"

Pandemonium broke loose in the crowded room.

Perry Mason turned to Rodney Cuff, made a little deprecatory gesture and said, "And there, Counselor, is your murder case!"

The entire end of the room where Weyman was struggling to escape became a seething mass of spectators. The coroner abandoned any attempt to secure order. The jurors themselves surged from their seats and joined in the melee. Perry Mason looked at his wrist watch, grinned at Coroner Scanlon, and said, "Thanks, Coroner, for the co-operation. I have fifty-seven minutes within which to go to my office, pick up my passport, and catch my boat for Honolulu, the Orient, Bali, Singapore, and wayplaces."

CHAPTER SIXTEEN

PERRY MASON'S powerful roadster roared into pulsating speed, as the car swept down the road from Los Angeles to Wilmington.

"Well," he grinned, looking at his watch, "we can just about make it—with luck. But we'll be starting out with just the clothes we stand in. We won't have any baggage aboard. It's a shame all that new baggage of yours is going to be wasted."

"Oh, no, it isn't," Della Street said. *"Our baggage* is all aboard."

"It's what?" Mason asked. "You mean—"

"Keep your eyes on the road," she warned.

"What's the catch?" Mason asked.

"No catch at all," she told him. "You told me to fill that baggage with bricks, old shoes, or anything else. I saw no reason why I should do that, so, instead, I filled it with all my personal belongings. When I took it out of the apartment house I didn't tell the transfer man to take it to the Trader's Transfer Company, but told him to take it directly to the *President Monroe*. Just so Sergeant Holcomb *thought* it had gone to Trader's Transfer Company was all that was necessary. And as for *your* baggage, I hired a valet to go out to your flat, pack up what you needed and ship it. I thought you'd neglect to do it."

"Good girl," Mason said, "I should have known you'd think of all the things I forgot— And so Holcomb *thought* the baggage was at Trader's. I'm a little rusty about what happened after that because I was stacking the cards to have the inquest go the way I wanted it. What's the lowdown?"

"Well," she reported, "Sergeant Holcomb went tearing down to the Trader's Transfer Company, hot on the trail of some baggage with the initials 'D.M.' on it. He found the baggage all right, and the more Trader tried to tell him it wasn't mine, the more he thought Trader was in league with you. So he became pretty hostile and smashed open the baggage. He found a lot of property which had been surreptitiously moved from some of the buildings which had been fired by this gang of incendiaries. Of course, he didn't know what it was at the time, but all of the fur coats and things made him suspicious. So he got in touch with the detective division and they identified the property in short order. So naturally, Sergeant Holcomb arrested me, and Judge Summerwaite signed the writ of *habeas corpus* and I got out just about the time Trader made some incriminating admissions."

"Did Trader implicate Weyman?"

"Not by the time I'd left. He did implicate Prescott and this Diana Morgan. Now, suppose you be nice to a poor working girl and satisfy *my* curiosity as to what happened, and then give your undivided attention to your driving. Personally, I want to catch that ship."

"Well," Mason said, "it all started when I got to figuring the thing from the standpoint of psychology. I figured that Walter Prescott had the psychology of a murderer rather than that of a victim, so starting my reasoning in that goofy way, I got to wondering who his victim could possibly have been. And I began to think of Carl Packard's disappearance. Then, suddenly, I saw a great light. Suppose Walter Prescott, as an insurance adjuster, had been standing in, either with or without Wray's knowledge, with a gang of incendiaries. It would make a perfect set-up, and it wouldn't have been the first time such a thing had happened. And if Packard had suspected Prescott, and was getting hot on the trail, Prescott would have been just the type to bump him off.

"But Carl Packard, who was a logical victim, *couldn't* have been a victim because he'd shown up at the hospital and made a voluntary statement that the accident had been his fault; that he'd been looking at something he saw in the window—and then the whole thing clicked in my mind.

"Packard was getting close on the trail of the real firebugs. They decided to murder him in such a way it would be virtually impossible to bring home the murder to them. You can see what happened: Weyman, one of the conspirators, let the gang beat him up enough so that he looked as though he'd sustained minor injuries in an automobile accident. Then, when Packard started out for Walter Prescott's house, Harry Trader, with his big van, followed along behind, and, at the proper moment, smashed Packard into the curb. He promptly unloaded Packard, put him in the covered van—and note that the covered van was an important factor in the conspiracy— and hustled off toward a hospital. The next time we contact the injured man is when he appears in the hospital. But, just as a stage magician frequently substitutes watches when he's walking from the audience up to the stage, so the victims were substituted during that journey in the covered van.

"The more I thought of it, the more I realized how perfectly plausible such a murder would be. Jason Braun, alias Carl Packard, was put into the van in an unconscious condition. He may have been dying then. For all we know, he was immediately the victim of the brutal assault which smashed in his head in such a way that identification became virtually impossible.

"When the covered van arrived at the hospital, Weyman, feigning unconsciousness, took Jason Braun's place and was carried out on the stretcher.

"Now then comes the masterly touch. Jason Braun was to disappear permanently. The conspirators wanted to make it seem that there was nothing suspicious about his disappearance. Therefore, they pulled that traumatic amnesia business, and Dr. Wallace fell for it, hook, line and sinker. He patched up Weyman's face, and Weyman came back to his house, having poured a little whiskey on his garments, taken a few drinks, and put on the act of having been drunk and fighting again.

"Now, when he arrived at the house, his wife told him of the latest gossip of the neighborhood; of what Mrs. Snoops had seen in Walter Prescott's house.

"Weyman immediately realized what a wonderful opportunity it would be to murder Prescott and get away with it. And Prescott was a thorn in the flesh of the incendiaries. For the one person who we absolutely *know* Jason Braun suspected in connection with this gang of firegugs was Walter Prescott. The conspirators were afraid that if Braun knew Walter was tied up with them, other people might know it. And they also knew that if Walter were arrested, he'd implicate them.

"As a sheer coincidence, and part of the act which the conspirators had put on at the hospital, Weyman, posing as Packard, had stated that the accident was his fault because his attention had been distracted by something he saw in the window of the house.

"So Weyman dropped over to call on Walter Prescott,

who had gone to his house following the accident, after the departure of his wife, and prior to the arrival of Rita Swaine. Weyman put on gloves, took the gun from its hiding place, approached Walter Prescott casually, under the guise of friendship, and fired three shots into him before Prescott knew what was happening, then returned the gun to its hiding place, and left the house.

"You see, the crime *must* have been committed *after* Jimmy Driscoll gave that gun to Rosalind Prescott. That is, if we're to believe Wray's testimony. And there's no reason why we shouldn't. In other words, Prescott was alive at eleven fifty-five. Virtually every minute of Driscoll's time is accounted for after that. Of course, he *might* have left the telephone and killed Prescott. But I couldn't figure him as Prescott's murderer because of things entirely foreign to the time element.

"Notice the manner in which Prescott was killed: He was killed in his bedroom. He was killed with no evidence of struggle. He was killed by someone, who, under the guise of friendship, was able to walk quite close to him, produce a gun and fire three times before Prescott realized he was in any danger.

"Prescott had previously mentioned to the police that someone had been prowling around the house, and, he thought, intended to kill him. It's quite possible that he had seen Braun while that individual was making some preliminary investigations. In any event, Driscoll, who was his sworn enemy, could not have approached him in the limited time which Driscoll had within which to act, and fired the fatal shot—not in the bedroom of his own house. Prescott would have been too much on his guard, too hostile. No, Prescott was killed by a friend, someone he trusted.

"Rita Swaine *could* have done it. Stella Anderson *might* have done it. Mrs. Weyman *could* have done it. None of those three really *would* have done it. Rita wouldn't have taken the gun from its hiding place after she had gone to so many pains to let Mrs. Snoops see her in the solarium. Mrs. Snoops and Mrs. Weyman could have

had no possible motive for the murder. None of the
three could have approached Walter in his bedroom without arousing Walter's suspicions.

"There was only one other person who knew that the
gun was hidden in that place, and that was Weyman.
His wife must have told him, and asked him what to
do, whether to call the police, and so forth. Thinking the
thing over, it all became perfectly clear.

"Having reasoned that far, and assuming that Prescott
was in a conspiracy to get places of business heavily insured, remove the most valuable goods from the buildings, fire them, and subsequently, as an adjuster, hold
up the insurance company for a splendid settlement, I
realized that the gang must have some way of disposing
of the goods.

"The redhead in Prescott's office looked like a phony
to me. In other words, she didn't look the part of a
legitimate stenographer, secretary and receptionist. As
soon as an investigation disclosed that she was leading a
double life, I knew I was right. As Diana Morgan, a rich
divorcee who traveled about the country, she was in a
position to have boxes and bags brought to her apartment, taken out by Trader, and eventually dispose of the
merchandise. Her apartment in the Bellefontaine made
an excellent place in which to hide and sort over the
loot. Later on, when the conspirators were ready to dispose of it, they could move it out, all packed in trunks,
bags and boxes."

"How about Jimmy Driscoll?" Della asked.

"Driscoll," he said, "or Rodney Cuff, his lawyer, or
both, evidently had some inkling of what was going on. I
think Jimmy tried to implicate Rita in order to free himself and Rosalind, so the two of them could work to
bring about a solution of the case. Unfortunately, I won't
have time to conduct any post-mortems on the clues with
Rodney Cuff. However, that young man apparently has
considerable on the ball. He figured out just about what
had happened all the way along the line."

"Then," Della said, "Weyman and Trader must have

stolen a car, taken Jason Braun's body out into the Santa Monica Mountains, wrecked the car, and left the body in such a manner that the features were practically unrecognizable. Is that right?"

"That's right," he said, "only I think what happened to Braun's features took place in the covered van on the road to the hospital. It isn't a nice thing to think about."

They drove in silence for a couple of miles. Then Della Street said, "Why did you want Sergeant Holcomb to get into that baggage?"

"Because," he said, "I figured we needed proof. I didn't want to start exposing Weyman until I had something definite. Weyman was so clever he acted the part of a surly ox and fooled me. When I realized the truth, I thought he'd dodge the subpoena and it would be necessary for me to make some accusations in open court. You see, Weyman had absolutely nothing to fear from any person in the world except one man. That man was Dr. James Wallace. Knowing that Dr. Wallace would probably be a witness at the inquest on Jason Braun's body, I couldn't believe that Weyman would have the audacity to show up. But that's where Weyman was more clever than I gave him credit for. You see, if he'd refused to obey the subpoena, that would have been an incriminating circumstance in itself. So Weyman outsmarted everyone by claiming that his face had become infected, and bandaging it in such a way that no one could recognize him.

"I thought, of course, that after Holcomb had once got on the trail, he'd shake down Trader and Rosa Hendrix until he got all the dope. But, by that time, our ship would've sailed. If Weyman showed up at the autopsy, I wanted to make a spectacular, whirlwind finish. I explained to Scanlon generally what I was working on, and Scanlon agreed to give me a free hand, within reasonable limits."

"Why didn't you go to Holcomb and tell *him?*" she asked.

Mason chuckled and said, "In the first place, Holcomb

would have tried to grab all the credit, and, in the second place, he wouldn't have co-operated. I could never have got him to search the luggage of Diana Morgan if it hadn't been for making him think that baggage contained stuff which would implicate you and me."

"How did you happen to suspect Weyman as the guilty party, Chief?"

"To begin with, he and Prescott both moved into the neighborhood at the same time—six months ago. Knowing that if a switch of victims had been made in that van, the man who went to the hospital must have had medical treatment, and remembering what Dr. Wallace had said about the injuries being facial and superficial, the wonder of it is that I didn't suspect Weyman before."

"Was Trader in on Prescott's murder?" she asked.

"No. He knew nothing about it until later, because he went right ahead and delivered the stuff to Prescott's garage. Then, learning of the murder, and knowing the police would search the garage, he sneaked the stuff up to Diana Morgan's apartment, to take it out last night concealed in inexpensive trunks and suitcases which would enable it to be shipped."

She frowned thoughtfully, then asked, "Why did Weyman support Driscoll by swearing he'd seen him at the telephone?"

Mason laughed. "Because he was clever as hell. He didn't care about Driscoll, but by swearing, apparently unwillingly, that he'd been standing where he could see Driscoll, he gave himself an alibi for the time of the auto accident, just in case anyone should get to wondering. It was a clever move. You see, he told his wife all about it, knowing she'd tell Mrs. Snoops, and knowing Driscoll's lawyer would interview Mrs. Snoops. The way he staged it fooled everyone. I might have doubted whether it was Jimmy Driscoll he saw at the phone, but he planted his build-up so smoothly that until I went back to first principles I never doubted that Weyman was there on the street, instead of in the van."

"All right," she told him. "I know enough now to figure

it all out. If there are any loose ends I can tie them up myself. You pay attention to your driving."

Mason stole a glance at his wrist watch, frowned, and pushed the accelerator down close to the floorboards. "And how!" he said.

CHAPTER SEVENTEEN

THE *President Monroe* had blown its fifteen-minute whistle. One minute to go. All visitors had been ordered ashore. Dock-hands were standing at the gangplank, ready to take it up. The band was playing.

Clouds which had blanketed the bay earlier in the morning were lightening somewhat, with patches of blue sky showing through. Streamers of colored paper furnished ribbons of color which stretched from passengers on the upper decks to friends who had gathered on the dock to say farewell. The edge of the wharf was lined with people calling out good-natured banter to those who were standing at the ship's rail.

The uniformed officer who was importantly directing the parking of cars stifled a yawn. Half an hour before, cars had been arriving by the score. Five minutes later, they would be leaving in droves. Right now he had nothing to do, save push his chest against his uniform and strut importantly up and down the pavement.

He looked up as he heard the sound of screaming tires, the roar of an automobile. He raised his whistle to his lips, then jumped to one side to avoid being struck as a car skidded sideways, swung half around, and lurched to a stop.

Mason jumped out, yelled at him, "Park that car somewhere," grabbed Della Street, and, together, they raced up the gangplank just as the hoarse bellow of the ship's whistle aroused echoes along the waterfront.

The gangplank was pulled away. Lines were cast off. The lawyer and his secretary, breathless from their mad scramble, stood by the rail, laughing, panting, and looking down across the widening strip of oily water at the sea of upturned faces.

Suddenly Mason said, "Look down there, Della, over against post number seven."

Della Street followed the direction of his eyes. Rodney Cuff, Jimmy Driscoll, Rosalind Prescott, and Paul Drake were gathered together in a compact group. Drake spotted them just as Della Street looked. He said something to his companions, then raised his voice and yelled, "Perry! We burnt up the road to get here. A client of mine has a case he wants you to take. This is right down your alley. He has plenty of money and—"

"Not interested," Mason called back.

"You can come back with the pilot," Drake shouted, "and—"

"Not interested," Mason interrupted, waving his hand. "I have a date in Singapore with a lady."

Cuff shouted, "I wanted to congratulate you. You got out of the courtroom before I knew you were going. Wonderful work, Counselor."

"Thanks," Mason called. "Hey, Paul, tell your man to take his case to Rodney Cuff. Good-by! I'll send you a card from Waikiki!"

The big engines throbbed into vibrations as the ship gathered speed. Drake yelled something which was unintelligible. The dock with its human fringe of waving figures slipped astern.

Mason turned to Della Street. "How's that," he asked, "for keeping a promise?"

Her face flushed, her eyes starry, she looked up at him, the fresh wind from the harbor blowing her hair about her flushed cheeks.

"Swell," she admitted.

"Now," he said, "we are confronted with the problem

that all your baggage is initialed 'D.M.' What are we going to do about *that*?"

"Can't we have the initials erased?" she asked.

"Not very well," Mason said, his eyes twinkling. "They're stamped into the leather. I'll tell you what you *could* do, though."

"What?" she asked.

"If," he said, "you became Mrs. Mason, the initials would be perfectly all right. They would then stand for 'Della Mason' instead of 'Diana Morgan.' "

"Are you," she asked, "proposing to me?"

He nodded.

She looked thoughtfully down into the water, then raised her eyes to face him frankly.

"As your wife," she asked, "would I continue to be your secretary?"

"Hardly. I couldn't give you orders. It wouldn't set well with the clients. But you wouldn't need to work. You could have a car of your own and—"

"That's what I thought," she interrupted. "We're getting along swell the way it is. You'd establish me in a home somewhere as your wife. Then you'd get a secretary to help you with your work. The first thing you knew, you'd be sharing excitement and experiences with the secretary and I'd be entirely out of your life. No, Mr. Perry Mason, you aren't the marrying kind. You live at too high speed. You're too wrapped up in mysteries. I'd rather share in your life than in your bank roll."

"But think of all that baggage," he told her, sliding his arms around her waist. "It has those perfectly good initials, 'D.M.,' which we can't let go to waste."

She snuggled close to him. "No," she said, "I think my hunch is right, Chief. I think it would be better for me to remain Della Street and have the baggage wrong than to become Della Mason and have everything else wrong. But—well, I'll tell you what I'll do—ask me again in Singapore."

"It's a long ways between here and Singapore," he told her. "How about Waikiki?"

She laughed, flung back her head to catch the wind on her cheeks and forehead. "Always impatient," she said. "Come on. Let's walk the deck. I don't think you need a wife. But I know damn well you need a secretary who's willing to go to jail occasionally to back your play."

Arm in arm they started walking the deck. "Have any trouble with that *habeas corpus?*" he asked.

"Nuh uh," she said.

Another half turn in silence. "Happy?" Mason asked.

"Uh huh," squeezing his arm.

Like two happy children, they walked the deck. "Dammit," Mason said, frowning, "I wonder what it was that Paul Drake had. It's the first time I've ever known him to get excited over a case. It must be a humdinger—"

She placed her fingers across his lips. "Stop it," she ordered. "Quit talking about it, and quit thinking about it. If you so much as mention business on this trip, I'll take a separate ship and leave you to your own devices."

Mason held up his hands in grinning surrender and said, *"Kamerad!* You win!"

Thereafter, passengers getting their last taste of the cold wind which came tanging in from the sea, hurrying toward their staterooms to lay out light weight tropical garments in anticipation of the warm cruise ahead, smiled tolerantly as they saw the tall, distinguished man, accompanied by the capable, good-looking young woman, parading around the deck, as though it was a ceremonial march, and, as they walked, whistling *Hawaiian Paradise.*

Perry Mason mysteries by
ERLE STANLEY GARDNER

Published by Ballantine Books.
Available in your local bookstore.